Tainted

NENE CAPRI

STREET CHRONICLES

Join us on our social networks

Like us on Facebook: G Street Chronicles
Follow us on Twitter: @GStreetChronicl
Follow us on Instagram: gstreetchronicles

Tainted

Acknowledgments

All praises are forever due to most high, I am so grateful for all the blessings you give me daily. To my beloved, thanks for respecting my dreams. To my mom Birdie you are the best and your backbone is like stone, you have taught me to stick to my words and put in the work to make them materialize. Thank you, I love you. Dad because I am your twin I will always do my best to make you proud. Nana RIP knowing I am almost who you wanted me to be. I miss and love you. To my favorite cousin Princess you are my rock, thank you for always being there for me and supporting me. I love you.

To my Family, we have been raised to know that we have special gifts. We must stay tight and continue to help each other capture our dreams. Failure is not an option. Let's get it.

Personal thanks to Wahida Clark "The Official Queen of Street Literature". Thank you for giving me wings and teaching me how to fly. I promise you I will soar. I love you. WCP team, I love you with all my heart can't wait to drop The Pussy Trap 4.

Keith of Marion Designs you did your thing on this cover. Thank you for taking my concept and bringing it to life in a grand way. To all the editors and my number one pre-drop reader Kisha Steele. Thank you so much for your great eye and skill.

Cash thanks for all your help and encouragement, you

are truly honorable. Aaron lets go wonder twin. Nuance Art your graphics are bananas they better get at you.

George Sherman Hudson your mind is brilliant and I look forward to helping bring some of your visions to life. Much love. Shawna A. thanks for being a woman of your word and making me feel at home at G Street.

To my Chief Executive of Promotions at Boss Lady Publishing, Lissha Sadler. You are the best ever. I am more than grateful for all that you do for me. I pray that your hands receive many blessings. I love you.

To my team of Bosses, Toni Doe, Lenika, Masterpiece, Giles, Ashley Nicole, Brandi, Tonsie, Kenya, Wynter, Jess, Erica, Tanny, Cass, Leah, Kelley Trotman you rock, Latisha. If I forgot anyone please charge it to my head not my heart. Thank you to all my reading Bosses, I am more than grateful to have you grace my pages. I can only pray that I can always give you what you want. Much love always…#GStreetTrapin.

Dedication

To my Princess Khairah.
Thank you so much for all your patience and
sacrifice. Everything mommy does is for you.
I Love you.

PROLOGUE

"*Ahhh—Ahhh...*"
"*Sssss—keep that ass up. You know how I like this pussy.*"

The man's growl echoed through the room along with the sound of skin slapping skin. The little girl lay on a couch only ten feet away from her dad's squeaking bed. The only thing that spared her from seeing him having sex with his girlfriend was the fact that her head was turned towards the wall, but that didn't shield her ears. She lay in the semi-darkness, fear and nausea growing inside her, as the intrusive grunts and moans became louder and louder and her father's distinctive voice assaulted her ear drums.

The little girl was nine years old and very curious so, despite her fear, she slowly rolled over to see what was going on. The soft light that glowed from a lamp on the nearby nightstand illuminated the bodies on the bed. The child's eyes grew wide. A tiny naked woman was on her hands and knees at the foot of the bed with her ass up in the air. The little girl's father had the woman by the waist pulling her back and forth into him. He moaned louder with every thrust as his sweat dripped onto the woman's *bare back.*

The child couldn't help staring at his mammoth penis as it plowed in and out of the small woman's body. The woman made sounds of intense pleasure but, to the little girl, it sounded like she was crying out in pain.

The child cringed.

"Fuck me good, baby. Tear this pussy up. It's yours—it's yours," cried said the woman in a muffled tone.

The little girl's ears pounded and her eyes traveled to where the woman had the sheets clinched tightly between her teeth. In the dimly lit room, the two bodies appeared as one. Her father's slim, chocolate frame towered over the woman. His forceful movements caused his face to distort and his brow to wrinkle as he seemed to bludgeon the woman with his manhood. She was loving it but the child thought she was being murdered.

As the woman's body rocked with pleasure the child's body shivered out of fear. She wondered why the woman wasn't kicking, screaming, and scrambling to run. Finally, it occurred to her that the woman was enjoying it. Conflicted, she didn't know whether to continue watching or to squeeze her eyes shut and turn away. When she tried to turn back to the wall, her head wouldn't obey. She found herself paralyzed by her fascination.

The girl instinctively knew that grownups should not have been doing this in front of her, especially her daddy who was supposed to be her protector. As the thought contorted her face into a scowl, her father looked up and their eyes became locked. Her heart pounded in her small chest as if she had been caught doing something very bad.

"Turn your grown ass around!" he yelled not stopping

his stroke.

The woman's head followed the sound of his voice. "Oh shit," she said, startled. She tried to move away as she realized his child was awake and fully tuned in like cable TV.

"Throw that ass back at me," he snarled, slapping her cheeks hard.

"Glen, we can't be doing this in front of a kid," she protested displaying a touch of decency despite being drunk.

"Shut the fuck up and keep that ass in the air. She's not seeing nothing she won't have to learn how to do one day."

"I guess you're right," she giggled and then spread her legs wider to allow him deeper access. Her flash of decency evaporated like her sobriety often did.

The man grunted as he went balls deep and began moving back and forth in her wetness. The child on the sofa quickly closed her eyes and trembled slightly as her father's growl shook her spirit. After a few seconds, she dared to peek through the small slits in her eyes. Her father was still punishing the woman but he was staring right at her with a wicked smile that made her pee on herself.

The girl jerked her head away and squeezed her eyes shut so tightly that her head began to pound. Her heart beat quickly as it filled with both fear and disdain. She continued to lay there listening to him plow in and out of the little woman. Tears filled her eyes and stained her pillow as the beginning of hatred filled her soul. She wanted to blink her eyes and disappear but instead her innocence was shattered with every sound. The smile on her father's face promised something unfathomable; it haunted her mind as she tried to cover her ears with the palms of her hands.

Recent memories of uncomfortable baths made worse by his awkward touch that had turned her stomach with every unwanted motion accompanied by that grin— that frighteningly grin— that made her fear that there would be more than seconds of discomfort and pain. She was afraid that there would be many haunting days of hell.

Tears streaked her tender face as she lay there, crying and praying. She prayed that the lewd sounds would fade into the night and that the smile on her father's face really didn't mean what her young mind feared.

CHAPTER 1

The Chase

Eight years later…

Spring was turning into summer in Newark, New Jersey. Dudes were standing on the corners talking shit and cracking jokes. Kids ran and played in the street. And, of course, the young girls couldn't wait to throw on their best and model up and down the blocks competing for a bit of attention.

It was just another day in the hood as Naseem headed over to Orange, to hit his man Hennessey off with some work. When he pulled up on Day Street to handle his business with Hennessey, he saw that the same thing was popping off there as back in The Brick. Every hood was truly the same.

Naseem stood on Day Street across from the corner store talking to Hennessey and passing time as he waited for a call from his right hand man. He ignored the ratchet females that paraded by with their asses and titties hanging out looking to come up off a nigga's trap. Those bitches were cheaper than a C&C soda. They didn't warrant dick let alone some holla.

He had some business to straighten in a minute. It was the kind of shit that was going to get a nigga outlined in chalk but Naseem wasn't pressed. The nigga was committing suicide by fucking with him and his team.

Naseem had just texted his people to check the verdict when he heard an innocent giggle coming from across the street to his right. He turned and a pretty young lady caught his eye. She didn't look like she had just stepped off the stage at a strip club. Little mama was wearing a catholic school uniform. Her skin was caramel brown and smooth. She had shapely bowed legs and curves for days. Naseem licked his lips as a tiny smile spread across his thuggishly handsome face.

His smile widened when he observed that her hair was down to the middle of her back. Naseem loved shorties with long hair. Gripping a handful of hair while stroking deep from the back had become his thing. Naseem fell into a small trance as he took in her beauty. It was like they had switched identities; he was the impressionable school girl and she was the bossed up muhfucka out on the block making moves.

The mere thought of that caused Naseem to chuckle. He stroked the baby fuzz on his chin and continued to check her out. When her radar picked up his stare, she smiled at him with an innocence that made his gangsta-proven heart flutter—something that hadn't happened in years.

"This shit is mad crazy," Naseem mumbled to himself.

It wasn't just that she was beautiful. At twenty-one years old, Naseem had been off the porch since he was a ten-year old snot-nosed kid learning at the elbow of older street gods. He had been running up in grown, pretty ass bitches since he clocked his first band at eleven years old. Neither beauty nor booty was his weakness. Something in l'il mama's smile moved him. She was a gem amongst rough glass. Naseem couldn't just let her walk by.

"Yo, little mama. Let me holla at you for a minute," Naseem yelled out.

"Huh?" she replied. She was caught off guard as she crossed the street with her girl, Breonni.

"If you can 'huh' you can hear," he said with a sexy smirk as she passed him.

L'il mama rolled her eyes and walked into the store.

Breonni tipped her shades, looked over at Naseem, and twisted her lips. She was a cutie too, but Naseem wasn't beat for that fast ass attitude.

"We need to get his thirsty ass something to drink when we get in here," she spat as she pushed her shades back up and followed her friend into the store.

"Yo, who is that little hot ass in the catholic school uniform?" Naseem turned and asked Hennessey.

"Who? Little mama that just walked into the store?" Hennessey asked in a 'nigga you need to stop' attitude. Hennessey raised his black and silver flask to his mouth and took a swig.

"Muthafucka, don't play. Just tell me her name?"

"A'ight, nigga. Damn, don't catch your period. That's little Katina. Sheeit, she ain't no hot ass. Katina and her crew are on some virgin pact shit. Some prom night shit that they been holding down like champs." Hennessey paused and took another swig from his flask then continued. "As for the chick with her, I don't have proof but I got some serious doubts about her loyalty to the pact. So if you're trying to hit, that would be the one to shoot for."

"Fuck is wrong with your hearing, yo? I didn't ask about her friend."

Naseem looked down at an incoming message on his phone. He nodded then shoved the phone back into his pocket.

Hennessey laughed. He could hear the seriousness in his man's voice. "Son, mad niggas done tried to crack Katina's code. You can forget it. She ain't going," he said.

Naseem wasn't deterred. His wheels had already begun to churn. He looked Hennessey in the eye and said confidently, "That's because mad niggas don't know what to do with pussy waiting to be trained."

"Nigga, I ain't got time to be chasing no pussy. Pussy chase me and, when I stop for it, it needs to have a trick or two up its sleeve," Hennessey joked as his bloodshot eyes stared back at Naseem.

"I hear that slick shit, nigga. But you know like I know. If a bitch can perform a trick too good, her pussy gonna feel like another nigga's dick is still in it," Naseem shot him a jewel.

"I feel you, fam," Hennessey laughed and hit fists with him.

"Let me see if I still got it," Naseem said as he headed towards the store.

"You a crazy muthafucka," said Hennessey smiling at Naseem's cockiness.

"I'll be right back."

Naseem double timed it across the street.

Hennessey shook his head, leaned against the stoop in front of his trap spot, and watched as Naseem went to try his hand at lady luck.

The streets had taught Naseem to fear nothing. Opportunity was just another bitch waiting to be claimed. Those who hesitated were left with the crumbs that fell off of a boss nigga's plate.

Naseem was destined to eat with the best. He had gotten his come-up early, banging rocks down in the Weequahic section of Newark. He'd never gotten caught up so he thought he was invincible. Naseem stood at six-one, one hundred and eighty pounds with confidence for days, chiseled features, sexy brown eyes with long lashes, and a smile full of pearly whites. His baby face disguised the beast that could spring out the minute a fool violated but his swag was undeniable.

Naseem stepped into the store. He wore a pair of black jeans with a matching hoodie and a North Face vest with Timberlands. Naseem always got what he wanted so he felt every woman was his for the picking. Maybe those other niggas couldn't get at little mama but they weren't him.

He posted up near the doorway and watched as Katina moved from one spot to the next grabbing a few items along the way. When she approached the counter he headed toward her with a single purpose. *Ma, you about to be mine*, he thought as he made his move.

CHAPTER 2

Rapture

Katina placed a soda on the counter and looked through her small Gucci clutch. "Can I have an apple Jolly Rancher stick, Poppy?" Katina asked with an innocent voice that was barely above a whisper. She put her hand out to exchange money for the merchandise.

Poppy smiled at her trying to force eye contact as he reached over and grabbed the candy from a small plastic container next to the register. Katina noticed the lust in his eyes but paid him no mind. She had burst his little bubble too many times to count.

Just then, Naseem came up behind her and softly pressed her against the ice cream box just below the counter. He leaned in and put his mouth against her ear.

"Can I give you something long and hard?" he asked in a syrupy whisper.

Katina looked over her shoulder ready to cuss a nigga's ass out. When she realized who the sexy voice belonged to, a nervous blush came across her face. She didn't know what to say or do. She was stuck between two hard places.

"Excuse me. Can you please move back so I can get out?" she replied breathlessly. The way his body pressed against hers caused her to flush red with heat.

"You didn't answer my question," Naseem said looking down at her and licking his full lips.

"No. I don't accept things from strangers, but thanks anyway," she forced out.

"Strangers?" he echoed, "A'ight let's fix that. I'm Naseem. So, now that I'm no longer a stranger can a brother get to know you a little better?" Naseem breathed warm air onto her neck with every word.

"Well, Naseem, as close as you are you should know my social security number and blood type. Can you please move back?"

"Let me get your number and I'll move back," he said continuing his negotiation.

"If I give you my number do you promise to move?" she asked with a flirty attitude.

"Yup."

Naseem's soft lips and warm minty breath on her neck piqued her interest. She sucked her teeth and called out her digits. Naseem committed her number to memory until he could program it into his phone because at that moment he was enjoying the feel of her body too much to move.

Katina turned around slowly and looked up into Naseem's eyes. They were warm and inviting. His semi-hard dick was right at the base of her coochie and felt so good. The look in his light brown eyes and his sexy grin had her clit pulsating. She could have stood there looking at all that thuggish sexiness forever had he not broken the silence.

"I wanna eat you out," Naseem whispered softly.

Katina's mouth fell open.

Naseem smirked and his eyes danced with devilish charm. "Oh, my bad, baby girl. I meant to say take you out, not eat you out," he corrected and flashed an even bigger smile.

Katina felt energy rise from her coochie to her chest that sent fire throughout her body. She swallowed quickly and, with her eyes still locked with his, she said sarcastically, "Um hm, I just bet you did and I bet you ask a lot of girls out."

Naseem stopped smiling and replied, "No, just the grown and sexy ones. Can you handle going out with a grown man?"

Katina was at a loss for words. She wasn't used to exchanging slick comments with men. She usually just kept it moving. It was the first time a man had gotten that close to her and this one looked good from head to toe. He had her at hello. His Versace Blue Jeans cologne was intoxicating. Katina's lips parted a little as the thought of him having all that sexy on top of her caused her breathing to pick up just a bit.

Naseem flashed that irresistible grin and broke her train of thought.

"Hello. Is anyone home?" he asked.

Katina was embarrassed; she smiled and looked down allowing her long hair to flow over her face as if it were a shield.

"Yes, I think I will let a grown man take me out," she declared.

A loud voice brought Katina back to reality, "Damn Tina, why he all up on you like that?" Breonni said as she emerged from the back of the store with a sandwich in her hand.

"He claims he wants to take a sistah out." Katina answered smartly. She had gotten a little courage now that her girl was back.

"Well, shit. Your scary ass needs to let somebody take you out, dig you out, and eat you out if they feel like it."

"Bre!" Katina said as a blush came across her face.

"It's all good. I like Ms. Bre. I think my nigga, Long, might like her even more," Naseem said.

"Long? I know his mama didn't name him that. So, what's long about him? His tongue or his dick?" Bre asked boldly.

Katina almost hit the floor at Breonni's openness. Her head snapped to the side and she looked at Breonni with wide eyes.

"Damn, little mama, you off the meter. You going to have to find that out for yourself, but I know he's going to have fun helping you come to that conclusion," Naseem said.

"Oh, letting me cum to that conclusion. Well, tell that nigga to bring his 'A' game because you can't just spin, bend, and run up in this," she spat. She put her cherry lollipop in her mouth and rolled it around playfully.

With that, Breonni quickly gave him the once over to review the hood check-list: shoes, haircut, hands, and nails. If any one of those was busted on a dude, he could forget it. Naseem passed with flying colors. She knew that niggas like that traveled in packs and she was going to get her one. It was time to let somebody pop that pussy.

"Come on, Tina. We got to go. Did you give sexy the

digits?" Breonni asked as she placed her sandwich on the counter.

"Yes," Katina responded. She couldn't even look up. She was embarrassed plus she didn't want Naseem to think she was a hoochie.

Naseem put his hand up to her chin and slowly lifted her head. He looked at her like he was going to stick his tongue down her throat. In truth, he could not wait to do just that.

"So, I can call anytime?" Naseem asked. "I ain't got to worry about nobody do I?"

"No, you don't. You can call whenever you like."

"A'ight."

He called her number out to make sure he remembered it correctly.

"Yes, that's it," she smiled.

"I'ma call you around ten o'clock," he promised. Then, Naseem looked at Poppy. "Yo, let me get two Dutch's and pay for whatever they get and give little mama the change."

Naseem passed Poppy a fifty dollar bill purposely pressing his body against Katina as he did and inhaling the vanilla that rose off her skin.

Katina took a deep breath.

Naseem backed up and looked at her one more time. "A'ight, ma, peace out."

As Katina watched Naseem walk away, her heart ticked loudly in her chest. Breonni was talking but Katina had totally tuned her out as she watched him walk to his car.

"Damn, bitch. Did the nigga hit you with some fairy

dust?" Breonni asked waving her hand in front of Katina's face.

"Oh, I'm good. Come on," she fronted like she wasn't struck. All of the while her heart was doing cartwheels and her mind was repeating, *I cannot wait until 10:00.* Katina felt capable of floating home on a cloud.

Naseem's demeanor changed as soon as he stepped out the store and felt his phone vibrate in his pocket. He pulled his phone out and answered the call that he had been waiting for.

The few words that were uttered on the other end sealed a nigga's fate.

CHAPTER 3

Back to Work

Darkness had replaced daylight by the time Naseem got with Long and Flint. Together they picked up their hired assassin, Hammer, and the four of them snatched up their quarry. Naseem pushed the conversation he had with Katina out of his mind and murder became his single thought. Antwan, a nigga that held Naseem's and his crew's freedom and lives in his hand, had to be dealt with without hesitation.

Antwan had seen too much and said too little. The murder Naseem and his crew had committed would put them in grave danger with one of the most powerful drug dealers in Newark if it ever came out. The only reason Antwan didn't already have a headstone was because they had needed him alive until he led them to the dude who was with him that night. Antwan swore he didn't know the boy. No muhfuckin' witnesses. That was the code of the streets.

"Muthafucka, you think we playing?" Long barked as

he stood over Antwan with his sawed off pump. "We gave you a week to find out that nigga's name and your time is up. You was serving him that night so you have to know something about him."

"Why you willing to die to protect the next nigga's identity? You fear that nigga more than you fear us?" Naseem asked in a calm emotionless tone that caused fear in Antwan's heart.

"I don't know shit," he whimpered from his kneeled position.

Naseem stood on one side of the frightened boy with his arms folded across his chest staring down at him with eyes that could go from warm to cold in a fraction of a second. Right now, his eyes were frigid. Flint stood on the opposite side of their captive wearing a scowl on his face. Hammer, the fourth member of their crew, stood behind him. Each man wore all black, the exact same charcoal color of their hearts.

"This muthafucka lying. Y'all want me to blast his ass?" asked Flint who was running out of patience. One head nod from Naseem or Long and he was popping Antwan's whole fuckin' melon. He raised his gun to Antwan's forehead and itched to squeeze the trigger.

"Come on, man. I just need a little more time and I'll find out the nigga's name, where he lays his head...the whole nine. Fuck he mean to me? All he did was cop some weight from me I didn't know him. That's my word!" pleaded Antwan. Tears formed in his eyes. He misjudged Naseem as the compassionate one and looked to him for a reprieve.

"Muthafucka, don't beg! Be twenty-one about it. You

was in the wrong place at the wrong time that night. Tell us that's nigga's name or you're about to take your last breath," Naseem yelled as their helpless victim kneeled before them with his hands tied behind his back. The summer night's heat washed over them and the dim street light accented the fear in Antwan's face and the evil in Naseem's eyes.

The stage was set. There in the dark alley with only the faint sound of water dripping from a nearby drain, Antwan's fate was inevitable. Death had knocked on his door and Naseem opened it wide allowing it to take control of the house.

Flint and Long stood in front of the man with their merciless canons ready to roar. The heavy breath that left their lips pushed fear into Antwan's heart like bolts of lightning. He had been given two weeks to come up with the name they needed. His time had run out.

"I told you. I just need a little more time," Antwan cried as sweat rolled down the side of his face.

"Nigga, your time is up," Naseem said as he reached into his bubble vest pulling out his forty-five.

"Nas, please," Antwan pleaded.

"Fuck this nigga, Nas. He think we pussy," Long growled then smacked the terrified man in the back of the head with a tire iron.

Antwan's body buckled to the pain but he held his scream fearing the next blow.

"Nah, Long, let me get at this nigga," Hammer said pulling a long handle with a shiny silver metal tip from the inside pocket of his vest. Raising it high, he came down hard on Antwan's shoulder. The sound of Antwan's collarbone cracking echoed against the brick buildings on both sides of them.

"Ohhh, shit! Come on, man!" Antwan yelped. As his body tilted to the side, surges of heat jolted through him stealing the very thoughts from his mind.

"Talk muthafucka," Hammer yelled as he brought the hammer down on Antwan's other shoulder causing his body to shift and distort.

"Ham, please, I just need time!" he pleaded. Unyielding pain shot through his body and paralyzing fear pumped blood through his veins hard and fast. His teeth chattered together uncontrollably and agony consumed his very existence.

Antwan raised his head and implored Naseem with his eyes. He rotated his glance from Long to Flint as sweat and tears ran from his face landing in a small puddle below.

"We ain't got no more time for you, muthafucka," Naseem barked. He gave Hammer the nod.

Antwan struggled to break free with the last strength he could muster. Flint and Naseem stood back watching him attempt to slither away with his hands bound behind him. His futile moments brought sinister smiles to their faces.

Hammer grabbed Antwan tightly by the back of his neck and began beating him in the back of his head with the mallet. The crack of metal against skull made a sickening crunch-like sound but reaped the boy no mercy. Blood splashed all over Hammer's face and arms but he was oblivious to carnage. He swung the hammer until white skull showed through the huge bloody gashes in Antwan's head. He dropped the tool and wrapped his powerful arms around Antwan's neck then looked up at his boys with a diabolical grin on his face.

"Yeah, do that shit," encouraged Flint. He had no mercy for a bitch ass nigga. *Punk muthafucka should've gotten ghost if he didn't have any answers.*

Antwan was already half-dead with broken bones and his head cracked open, but with the little strength left in his battered body he tried to squirm out of the death hold.

Hammer laughed. "Wiggle all you want, muthafucka," Hammer taunted, "but it won't do you no good. I'm sending you to your maker tonight."

Antwan uttered an incoherent plea. Hammer gripped his head tightly and snapped his neck.

"Damn," Flint exhorted covering his mouth with one hand and grabbing his balls with the other, "that shit was wild, yo!"

Hammer released his grip and watched Antwan as his face slammed onto the ground.

"Blow that nigga's head off. He too stupid for brains," Long spat.

Flint picked up his pump and blasted what was left of Antwan's head all over the hot concrete. The four men stood for a few seconds looking at their victim then they stepped to the truck, jumped in, and peeled out. They were no closer to the answers they were looking for but neither was their enemy.

Flint drove in silence as his mind tried to wrap itself around the fact that there was still one other person alive that saw them commit the murder. None of them were safe.

CHAPTER 4

Attraction

Two weeks later…

It was Friday night and the club was jumping. The line was long and Evergreen Place was packed with cars and onlookers. Raven, Jovonna, and Breonni were smack in the middle of the line laughing and talking loud. They were all fresh in crisp tight jean shorts and tank tops. The J's on their feet looked like they had just fallen out of the box. For such short and petite girls they kept up a whole lot of noise. Katina was standing there giggling and shaking her head. She'd never get into their loud ass debates even though they were very entertaining.

"Nah, fuck that. I told that bitch her tight ass pony tail must be cutting off the air to her brain confronting me about some nigga she be necking off," Breonni said and slapped hands with Raven.

Jovanna stood back on her legs as their pretty red bone tone extended from her shorts. Her long brown wavy hair bounced. Her pretty dimples sunk in her cheeks as she smacked her lips and jumped in.

"Fuck that bitch. She fucking everybody. How she gonna confront you about some broke ass nigga? She better fall back," Jovonna said causing everyone to crack up laughing and agree with her.

"Y'all mouths are so dirty," Katina said as she smiled and shook her head. She was considered to be the baby of the crew and she held her position well.

"Shut your goodie two shoe ass up. I heard about you," Raven spat moving the hair from over her left eye.

"What?" Katina feigned ignorance.

"Bitch, don't play," Raven said crossing her arms in front of her.

"You know she's all shy and shit," Breonni said while sucking on her lollipop. "Girl, we were in the store a couple of weeks ago and this fine ass nigga came up on her putting his whole pimp game on shorty rock over here. And she was all goo goo, ga ga. Bitch was in a straight trance."

"Stop playing," Jovonna said, holding her stomach and laughing.

Raven chimed in, "Mother Teresa over here?"

"Whatever," Katina said pursing her lips. "Just because I don't give my number to every lame with a pulse don't mean I'ma square."

"Bitch, please you're two squares," Breonni clowned slapping hands with Raven.

"Oh, shit, give up more details," Raven said doing a little dance as if this was her hook-up. "Was he paid?"

"Nigga was glossy. I would fuck with 'em," Breonni admitted with no hesitation.

"He was alright." Katina shot her an admonishing look.

"We'll talk about that shit later. Let's check out these flossy niggas sitting on dubs." Breonni stuck her tongue out at her girl, quickly changing the subject sensing Katina didn't want to be put on blast.

The friends stood there talking and observing everyone who pulled up. Young hustlers rolled through teen club night in a variety of expensive whips. Most of the girls outside of the club were oohing and ahhing over the rides but Katina's mind was on Naseem. They had been talking on the phone almost every day and seeing him again stayed at the front of her mental.

All of their heads turned when twin BMW 6 Series pulled up across the street with music thumping loud enough to wake the dead. The rims on both whips shined like platinum. One of the cars was red. The other one was metallic blue and its paint job glistened.

"Dayam," Jovonna sang looking at the two sexy brothers who got out of the blue BMW.

"Oh, shit. That's him," Breonni said, elbowing Raven in the side. "That's Katina's boo."

Raven's eyes settled on the two ballers that her girl was pointing at.

"Which one?" She fought to contain her excitement.

"The one in front," Breonni said, pointing in the direc-tion of Naseem who was leaning against his car. His man who was riding with him posted up on the hood attracting a flock of groupie love. Two more brothers got out of the red Beemer that had parked next to Naseem. They, too, attracted mad females.

The four girls were fixated on the attention that the

men commanded from the small crowd that had formed around them. They watched one dude after another go up to Naseem and his crew, give them some dap, and lean in for brief, private conversations.

Naseem had told her that he was going to fall through. Now, Katina smiled shyly and butterflies filled her stomach as she backed up behind Raven. Talking to him on the phone was one thing. Kicking it with him in front of her girls was another. She was unaccustomed to this part of the dating game.

Breonni shot her eyes to the sky and said, "Bitch, don't hide. That nigga is eye hustling all over this piece."

Naseem noticed Katina from across the street. He walked away from his boys to head in their direction.

"Oh, shit, here he comes," Jovonna said. "He needs to bring his boys. There's four of them and four of us and a bitch don't believe in coincidence."

"Girl, shut your thirsty ass up," intoned Raven playfully.

"Correction," said Jovonna. "I'm not thirsty. I'm dehydrated."

Raven and the others laughed hard at Jovonna's silliness but none of them took their eyes off Naseem. That nigga lit up the lot. His long platinum chain swung side to side and the diamonds in his medallion sparkled in the night. When he reached the curb, he stepped right to Katina.

"What's up, little mama?" he asked.

"Nothing," she responded lowering her eyes.

"Can I have a hug?" he asked giving her that enticing smile and reaching for her hand.

Katina moved towards him and stepped into his arms. She pushed up on her tippy toes giving in to his strong embrace.

Naseem held her tightly and crooned in her ear. "Damn, ma, you feel good in my arms."

It felt good to Katina, too, but he had her on front street and that made her nervous. Very subtly, she tried to pull back.

Naseem held her tighter and drew her closer into his chest. His cologne made her weak. "You need to stop being scared of me," he teased as he watched her blush.

"I'm not scared of you," she said looking down.

Her girls were eating it up. Naseem's strong arms were tatted from wrist to shoulder. His dark blue Citizen Jeans sagged just right lying on top of his black boots.

As Katina rested her body against his, she remembered the pact that she and the girls made not to give up the pussy at least until prom night. She didn't know if the others were remaining true to their word, but Naseem's magnetism made her heart race. She wanted to do everything she said she wouldn't do.

Naseem kissed her gently on her forehead. "Come across the street for a minute. I want to introduce you to my people."

He took Katina's hand and started across the street without waiting for her response.

"Oh, so you don't see nobody else standing here?" Breonni asked with a cute little attitude.

"What's up short and feisty?" Naseem leaned in to give her a half hug with his other arm.

"Did you give your boy my message?"

"He's across the street. Come give it to him yourself."

"We'll be right back," she said to her girls as she walked

across the street with Katina and Naseem.

When they reached the car the smell of weed hit them in the face. Flint, Shawn, and Long were posted up with the music playing and looking at the two beautiful young females that Naseem had brought to the car.

"Long, this is Breonni," Naseem said. He pushed Breonni towards Long.

Long and Breonni took each other in and Naseem stepped behind Katina. He wrapped his arms around her waist and whispered into her ear as he nibbled on her neck. He was on the chase and she was loving every minute.

"You had something to ask me?" Long said.

He was checking her out. Breonni only stood at 5'1" and her tight shorts clung to her hips and small waist. His eyes traveled up her flat stomach to her perky breast. Her shoulder length hair framed her pretty mocha face. She was definitely something sweet in a tiny package.

Breonni removed the lollipop from between her lips and looked him up and down, too. She loved what she saw. Long stood a little over six feet tall. His dark Hershey chocolate complexion looked sweet enough to give a bitch a cavity. Breonni involuntarily licked her lips. He had the same sleeve tattoo as Naseem running wrists to his shoulders on both arms and the white tank shirt showed off all his glory. She was caught up for a minute.

Long watched her checking him out.

"You gon' answer my question?" he asked.

Breonni tore her eyes off of all that goodness. "Yes, I wanted to know what was long. Your tongue?" she paused to look at his mouth.

"Or your dick?" she continued looking down at his

crotch.

Breonni returned her gaze to his eyes and waited for his response. She rotated the candy in her mouth and sucked in her jaws.

"Oh, shit," Flint said. He couldn't believe this little hot mama was trying to spit game at his boy.

Long took a hard pull on the blunt, smiled at Breonni, and said, "All my shit long – my money, my tongue, and my dick."

Breonni removed the candy from her mouth smacking her tongue, "That's what they all say until they pull it out and come up short."

"Bre!" exclaimed Katina. She was embarrassed by her girl's straightforwardness.

"What? Sheeit, you know it's the truth. Niggas always say they got that beast then pull out a lamb."

Breonni looked over at Katina who just covered her eyes and put her head down. Katina couldn't help wondering how Breonni knew so much about a dude's dick size if she was truly holding down the pact.

Long grabbed her by the wrist and pulled her toward him. In one swift movement, he took her by the waist, turned her around, and placed her butt right on his dick.

"Ummm," Breonni moaned softly.

Long looked at Naseem and said, "I like her. Where you get her from, Ock?"

"I told you she was real with her shit," he replied squeezing Katina tightly.

Long gripped Breonni's hips and positioned his dick right between her butt cheeks and let it rise. As his length grew against her she took in a little air then wiggled. He held her securely in place keeping his hand on her body.

Moving her hair from her neck he whispered into her ear, "Is it long enough?"

"Time will tell."

She moved forward turning to face him. She reached into her pocket, pulled out her cell phone, and offered it to him.

"Let me get your sevens."

Long chuckled. He was certain this young girl had no idea what she was getting herself into but if she wanted some thug lovin', he was damn sure going to give it to her. He took her phone, programmed his number, and handed it back to her.

"Only call me when you really need something," he said.

"Oh, don't worry. I need it. And, you damn sure got it."

Breonni looked him over once more then said to Katina, "Let's go. We have a party to attend."

"Naseem, I'm going to have to go," said Katina.

"A'ight. Call me tonight."

Naseem turned Katina around, hugged her snuggly, and then released her.

"And don't make me have to fuck none of these little young boys up," he added holding one of her hands as Breonni pulled her by the other.

"Okay," she responded. Katina started giggling as Breonni pulled her across the street.

When they reached their girls, the two of them were talking, laughing and slapping hands on their way into the club.

"Them niggas are on point," Breonni said pulling out

her money.

"Yup, and we about to cuff they asses," Raven said looking back in Flint's direction.

Naseem took the blunt out of Long's hand, leaned against his car, and watched Katina and her crew sashay inside. He had to admit he was feeling shorty. He had promised himself that he would not allow the blood on his hands to drip into her front yard.

"Damn, Breonni hot," said Flint.

"Nah, not really," Naseem cut in. "I think she frontin'. They all some good girls. My nigga Hennessey told me they all virgins that have made a pact not to give it up until prom night."

"Damn, my nigga! Why you ain't put me down? That Nigga Long got more bitches than he can keep up with," popped Flint.

Naseem looked at him reproachfully. "Quit hatin', yo. Little mama got two more friends. It's four of them and four of us I'ma hook y'all up,"

"Virgin pussy? I don't know if I'm trying to chase that. I got too many bitches on my dick to be running behind a bitch that ain't gonna fuck. For real, yo, that bitch better be dimed up," Shawn said while staring at the screen of his cell phone.

Pretty boy Shawn rocked labels from head to toe. His light brown skin tone matched his light brown eyes. The very low cut and small wave pattern haircut was set off by the two big diamonds in his ears. The pretty muthafucka was definitely model material. Naseem would only fuck with him occasionally because sometimes his heart was as soft as baby shit.

"Bruh, the other two friends cuter than a muthafucka, too. Just chill, nigga. I got this."

Naseem pulled deeply then passed him the blunt.

"Anyway," he continued. "Me and Long about to go take care of that business."

"A'ight. We gonna hang here for a minute looking at jailbait," Flint joked bumping fist with Naseem.

"Keep this nigga calm," Flint said to Long bumping his fist.

"You know I got it under control," Long spat then hopped in the car.

"I'll hit you tomorrow afternoon," Naseem said. He jumped into the driver's side, cranked his music, and peeled off.

Flint and Shawn remained posted up outside the club. They were kicking it with a few dudes and watching the action when chaos broke out across the street.

Flint zeroed in on the girl in a full-blown argument with a dude who appeared to be getting ready to smack the shit out of her.

"Is that Nadiyah?" he elbowed Shawn.

"Hell, yeah," Shawn said as he took off across the street.

Flint killed the engine and followed him.

"What the fuck is going on?" Shawn stepped to the shorty with tats all over his face.

"Nigga, this ain't your business," he shot back with a growl.

"Muthafucka, that's my sister you trying to lay hands on," Shawn moved a little closer to him.

"I don't give a fuck," little nigga spat back as the crowd

began to gather around them.

"Hold the fuck up," Flint stepped in and gave little man the death eye. "My nigga, you need to calm down."

"Shawn, grab Nadiyah and put her in the car."

Shawn snatched up his sister and damn near dragged her from the middle of the chaos.

Turning his attention back to the wanna be gangsta, Flint began to do what he does best – put a nigga in check.

"Now, I don't know what happened and, to be honest, I don't give a fuck," he spat moving dangerously close to ol' boy. "I'ma give you a pass tonight because leaving behind witnesses is not my get down. Plus, I know you ain't trying to die over no fifteen year old pussy. You feel me?" Flint glared down at him unwaveringly.

"That bitch robbed me," Paco stated in a stern but much calmer tone knowing that Flint's question was more than just a warning.

"Well, her debt is now my debt. How you wanna settle it?" Flint said reaching in his pocket.

Paco looked up in Flint's cold eyes. The attention from the crowd made his pride want to jump but his mind told him he better shut the fuck up.

"We good, my nigga," Paco said throwing his hands up.

"You're dismissed," Flint spat holding firm eye contact.

Paco backed up slow. All eyes were on him as he climbed into the car and closed the door.

Flint gave him a final warning. "This shit is over playa."

He reached into his pocket, pulled out a knot, and threw it on the front seat.

"Be easy," Flint spat as Paco pulled off.

Shawn raced up to the curb and popped the locks.

"Damn, that nigga a beast," a young girl on his right said.

Flint turned and gave her a wink as he jumped into the car and sped off.

As Shawn zipped through the streets, he thought about the close call they had just had. Most of his troubles stemmed from him trying to protect his baby sister. How much longer would he be able to shield her before her grown ass antics caught up with her?

CHAPTER 5

Loyalty

As they travelled through the Holland tunnel, Long and Naseem focused on their upcoming meeting. Long was cool but Naseem was slightly conflicted. It had been damned near six years since he saw his brother. Prison had not only separated them physically but it had placed a barrier between them and had damaged the brotherhood that they once thought was impenetrable. Naseem caressed the leather on the steering wheel as he rounded each corner on the way to the pool hall.

Long noticed the stress on Naseem's face and knew that he was trying to come to terms with his relationship with his brother. Still, Naseem needed to settle down. They needed a supplier and turning back was not an option. The city was drying up and they needed this connection to get things back on track.

"You good?" Long asked.

Naseem looked over at his boy then responded. "Yeah, I'm straight."

"We need this shit but if you ain't straight then I'ma be

more than uncomfortable. We riding on this together. Just say the word."

Long stared at the side of Naseem's face waiting for a small sign that shit wasn't right.

"Nah, we good." Naseem said as he kept his eyes focused on the small groups of people moving from one corner to the next.

"A'ight," Long affirmed as he turned to look back out over the city.

Naseem pushed the whip into the lot next to the pool hall and killed the engine. Before exiting the car, they checked their guns and adjusted their minds to business mode.

Long cautiously scanned the area as they approached the door. They knocked three times, stepped back, and waited for the door to open. A minute later Naseem's brother's right hand man answered.

"Oh, shit! A muthafuckin' ghost," Chucky slurred as he extended his hand to Naseem.

"What's up, my nigga?" Naseem said with a slight smile on his face as he gave him some dap.

"Sheeeit. I can't call it," Chucky said as he pulled him in and they bumped shoulders. Releasing Naseem, he turned his attention to Long.

"What's up, baby boy?" he greeted him.

"Just trying to live, my nigga," he moved forward and gave him the coded hand shake.

"He's waiting on you in the back," Chucky informed Naseem.

Refocusing his attention to his partner, "Long, you can come enjoy some of this New York hospitality," Chucky said extending his hand to display the roomful of women and money.

Long's gaze wandered over the many pool and card tables and then settled on the women who were giving sensual lap dances in the back. The music and the black and silver decor put his mind at ease.

"Yeah, a nigga needs to increase his bank roll and if I can enjoy something sexy while I'm doing it that's even better," he responded as his eyes fixated on some long, shapely caramel legs.

"Enjoy yourself. Nas will be right back," Chucky nodded at the security that got on point and led Naseem to the back.

Baseem looked up from his big, black desk as Naseem was led inside. When his eyes met Naseem's they shared a few seconds of uncomfortable silence. Security closed the door and posted up right outside.

"It's been a long time," Baseem's deep voice echoed throughout the room.

"Too long," Naseem responded. He felt as if his feet were rooted in place. He was not really secure about where he stood in his brother's world.

Baseem rose to his feet and moved towards his baby brother.

"Nigga, I damn near changed your diapers. You better act like you know."

Baseem walked up to him and stood only inches away. Naseem put out his hand. Baseem grabbed it and pulled him into an embrace. After a few seconds, they pulled back and made eye contact.

"We good?" Baseem asked.

Naseem nodded as he felt the lump forming in his

throat. Baseem was more than a brother to him. He had raised and protected him after their parents were killed. They were all they had. The fact that he had dropped the ball when Baseem went down hurt him to his heart. Baseem could see it in his eyes.

"The past is the past. We move on from here. Nothing can change that your blood is my blood," he affirmed.

He stared deep into Naseem's eyes making sure that what he read was real. What he saw in his little brother's eyes was not only admiration but loyalty as well.

"You all I got," Naseem confessed staring back into his brother's eyes.

"I got you," Baseem said.

Baseem released Naseem's hand and moved back to his seat behind the desk.

"Be seated," Baseem said as he sat down and lit up.

Naseem took a seat in the chair in front of the desk and, without hesitation, got straight to the point of his visit.

"You are the only one I feel safe to come to," Naseem said as he took the blunt from Baseem's hand.

"Hold up," Baseem stopped him with a hand in the air. "Before we move forward, is there anything that will interfere with business?"

Baseem asked looking in his brother's eyes for any deceit in his answer. Naseem thought about the unfinished business of finding the one person who could link his crew to the murder. If that ever came out it would cause hell for everybody associated with them, including Baseem. He thought about telling his brother but Naseem figured that was his problem. He would settle it long before things between them were set in stone.

Smiling confidently Naseem replied, "Nah, we good. There is nothing standing in the way of business. Nothing at all."

As the words passed his lips, guilt settled into his chest. They were just putting the past behind them and he had managed to sneak some deceit into their new accord.

The brothers passed the blunt back and forth while Naseem brought Baseem up to speed on the turmoil in the city. The death rate was climbing and the food chain had a snag in it causing a drought that had niggas' pockets bleeding. Baseem began to put a strategy together that would be beneficial to both of them. Naseem listened intently.

"It's that bad in Newark?" Baseem asked, inhaling deeply.

"Hell, yeah. That nigga, Nard, and them got the city hot as a muthafucka," he reached out for the blunt and placed it to his lips.

"Damn. And that nigga, CJ, killed himself?" Baseem asked, shaking his head. "They needed to put that bitch, Tamika's, pussy on a mantel. She had niggas on suicide watch," he chuckled. Baseem sat back and folded his hands on his chest.

Naseem chuckled as he continued to puff. "Yeah, them niggas wildin'. They got every thug in the city in tears and got the work slow as hell," he reported, reinforcing his need for his brother's help.

"Not tears, l'il bruh?" Baseem said and burst out laughing. "Fuck going on? Thugs cryin'?"

"Hell, yeah. Them niggas got the game fucked up."

Naseem relaxed as he felt the ice breaking between them. He got comfortable in his seat and waited for his brother's response.

Baseem stared past Naseem as he thought about what they were about to embark on together. Baseem was used to playing with the big boys, but this was going to be new for Naseem. Peeling his eyes from the wall, he looked into Naseem's face and gave it to him straight, no chaser.

"You know I handle mine and I will put my life on the line for you but you're stepping into a whole new game. The players on this side will kill everything you love if they suspect any cross in your blood," Baseem leaned forward stared into Naseem's eyes.

Naseem didn't blink and his voice didn't shake when he replied.

"You know I am as thorough as they come. My word is all I have and I stand firm behind it," he vowed unwavering to the loyalty backing his claim.

As he spoke, Naseem thought about his brother's mistakes and how forgiving him had taken six years. Still, the fact remained that no matter what had happened in the past their love and brotherhood would crush any doubt or disdain.

"I hope so. I love you with everything that I am but I don't do bitch niggas or snitch niggas. If anything folds, you better fold with it," Baseem warned.

"You already know."

"Time will tell."

Baseem hoped Naseem understood what he was getting into.

"So, do you think I will be able to have a sit down with

Kayson?"

"Right now, you just sit down with me. If he feels the need, he will send for you. I will contact you in a couple days with the time and place of pick up," Baseem answered as he rose to his feet.

"Thank you, big bruh. I won't let you down," Naseem said.

Baseem gave him a slight smile and said, "You know I could never tell you no."

"I love you 'til the death of me," Naseem proclaimed.

"And, I love you past the grave. We all we got. Don't disappoint me."

Baseem put his hand out to seal the deal.

"I got you," Naseem confirmed.

"A'ight let me take you out here to enjoy these little freak hos," Baseem said leading the way to the door.

"I'm not trying to go home with my dick in my pocket," Naseem joked.

Baseem shook his head and teased, "Nigga, you still scary as hell."

"Hell, yeah. I need this muthafucka for something," he laughed and grabbed his dick.

"Nigga, please. If that little muthafucka fall off, you ain't gonna be missing nothin'," Baseem shot back.

"But yo bitch might be upset," Naseem quickly responded.

"Oh, shit. Well, she out here. Let's go find out."

They burst out laughing and headed to the main area.

For the rest of the night, Naseem, Long, and Baseem tossed around a few strategies and enjoyed the festivities the pool hall deemed freak night. They parted company in the wee hours of the morning.

Baseem headed to his office with Chucky on his heels.

"You think Kay gonna be cool with Naseem running Jersey?" Chucky asked.

"I'm not sure yet but we gonna put him to the test. I love my brother with everything that I am but if he fails, Kayson won't have to come for him because I will take his life myself."

Chucky knew that Baseem wasn't just talking. With him, murder was like breathing. If a nigga inhaled the wrong way he would make it his last breath, brother or not.

CHAPTER 6

A Man's World

After his rendezvous with the stripers at his brother's pool hall, Naseem decided that he'd had enough of fast assed, gold digging bitches. With a new connect and product moving at a rapid pace, he needed to tighten his circle and put a woman in his bed who would be an addition to his collection of great things. He promised himself that was the last time he would be fucking with those types of thirsty hos. Naseem needed to have a rider by his side, a woman he could train to do what he liked and what he said. Katina quickly came to mind. She had been coming to mind often.

He pulled himself out of bed, showered, and threw on some fresh gear. After counting and organizing a few stacks, he grabbed his daily play money then headed out the door to scoop Katina up. He decided to leave his Beemer. Instead, he rolled in his Infiniti QX56. After taking her to get something to eat, they drove up to Short Hills Mall where copped her something pretty for her wrist. Katina realized that it did no good to protest. Naseem liked to buy her things and there was no way to stop him. She had to admit that he made her feel special.

Katina smiled all the way home looking at the iced up bracelet that wrapped comfortably around her tiny wrist. Naseem smiled when he saw the glint in her eyes. He had to quickly secure his spot in her heart because he had moves to make and needed her tight in his corner.

At the Colonnade apartment buildings in Newark, Naseem parked his truck, jumped out, and went to open Katina's door.

"Thank you for the dinner and my gift. I love it and I had a nice time," Katina said as Naseem took her hand to help her out.

As she slid down from the high sitting truck Naseem was right there to catch her in his strong arms. It gave her another preview of that hard candy he planned to hypnotize her with. Katina was stuck once again between two hard spots. She was happy to be there but, at the same time, was scared as hell.

Naseem looked deeply into her eyes while rubbing his hands up and down her back. Katina felt like he could read her thoughts, so she kept looking away to decrease the intensity of the moment.

"Why you shaking?" he asked.

Katina looked down at Naseem's semi-hard dick and back up at him.

Naseem said, "Oh him? He don't bite. I got him trained. He's a good boy."

Shit it feels like he does more than bite she thought. All she could say was, "Yeah, right."

Naseem smiled, "Come upstairs with me for a minute.

Then, I'll take you home. I have to get something."

Now, Katina was petrified. She had never been in a boy's house before. *What is he going to expect from me?* she thought. She walked beside him and each step felt like she was stepping closer to her own execution. By the time they reached the elevator she could hardly breathe.

"Don't look so worried," Naseem said, "I would never do anything to you that you are not comfortable with."

He pushed his floor number while holding her right hand firmly in his.

By the time they reached his floor, Katina had started to relax. After all, Naseem hadn't done anything up to this point to make her not trust him. Naseem took out his keys, opened the door, hit the lights and walked in. Katina was surprised by how clean and orderly his place was.

"Have a seat on the couch. I'll be right back," he instructed then headed to his bedroom.

Katina admired his color scheme of black and tan with touches of green. The tan suede sofa hugged her body like a pair of arms she sat enjoyed the view of the city from the window which was from floor to ceiling with no blinds or curtains. The black plush carpet was about three inches thick. She wanted to take her shoes off and just walk back and forth. She posted up by the window and stared at the lights of New York in the distance.

Naseem emerged from the back, "You want something to drink before we leave?"

"No, thank you. I'm fine," she said as she turned in his direction.

"You ready to go?"

"Yes, I have practice in the morning."

"Practice for what?"

"Piano."

"You play the piano?" he asked surprised.

"Yes, since I was seven. I'm going to college on a music scholarship and I have a final solo next week."

"Oh, okay. What do you want to be?" he asked leaning up against the counter.

"A psychologist. The human condition in connection with the mind is so complex. I want to see how it works."

"Damn, ma, you got it all planned out. Let me be your first patient. What am I thinking?"

Naseem stood a few feet away but the intensity in his eyes made her heart skip.

She paused and thought for a minute. "You're thinking that I am very pretty and you want to kiss me," Katina said with that sexy, shy tone. She knew that she was taking a chance by saying that but she wanted to taste his lips. They looked so good.

"Well, I think you're going to do very well in your field," Naseem said as he walked toward her and reached for her waist. When he leaned in and placed his lips softly on hers, he heard a slight moan.

He parted her lips with his tongue and started to kiss her passionately. Katina's mind raced and her body felt engulfed in flames as his hands roamed up and down her butt. He was firm, yet gentle. Goosebumps formed on Katina's skin as his touch sent chills through her body. Hesitation almost blew the moment but her curiosity took over allowing her to relax and enjoy the precision of his fingertips.

When Naseem started kissing her neck, Katina leaned

her head back. *What is he doing to me?* rang loudly in her head. For the first time, she was experiencing the things her older sister told her felt so good. Katina broke the moment and tried to back up a little but Naseem got closer.

"You all right?" he managed to say in between kisses.

"Yes. I'm fine. It's just that I have never been kissed before."

Katina avoided his gaze and fidgeted with her fingers.

Naseem paused for a minute and looked closely at her to see if she was serious.

"You for real?"

"Yes, I'm for real," she folded her arms over her chest. "I don't just go around kissing random dudes, but it's something about you."

"You want me to stop?"

"No, it's not that."

She nervously fidgeted with her shirt.

"I want to be here with you, but I don't want you to think that I'm easy."

She looked into his eyes then looked down.

"Plus, I will admit I am a little scared."

Naseem placed his finger under her chin and lifted her head. Locking eyes with her, he felt all her innocence at that moment. This was confirmation of what his boy, Hennessey, had told him about her being a virgin. Naseem would never have guessed that she'd never even been to first base.

"You never been kissed before?"

"No. I am a complete virgin," Katina said and put her hands out to the side.

Naseem's dick started to jump. He had to calm old boy

down as his eyes roamed over her breast. He performed serious mental gymnastics to get his body and mind on the same page. His body was desperate to have her but his better judgment told him not to rush.

Katina folded her arms in disappointment. She thought the revelation that she was a virgin had caused him to suddenly lose interest. She had no idea that it was the complete opposite. Naseem actually was trying to keep from attacking her.

"What's the matter, ma?" he asked responding to her sudden mood change.

"Nothing. I am really hoping that this doesn't make you leave me alone."

Her soft voice carried her sweet words to his eardrum.

"Ever since that day in the store, I could not get you out of my mind. I have never been this close to a man and you produce feelings in me that I have never felt."

Normally, those words would have had Naseem ready to ride but Katina had some special qualities that he needed in his life. He was determined to nurture her right and mold her into that loyal woman that he needed by his side. He was thrown totally off his game because here he had a young girl talking to him like a grown woman. Her firm eye contact and sincerity behind her words made him feel like an inexperienced young boy.

Katina thought that she had blown it. She knew that grown men liked women that do grown up things. She had no idea that wasn't always the case. Most street niggas dreamed of having a beautiful young virgin, something the next nigga did not have. Naseem wanted to be the first one to enjoy all the passion that she would give him once he was deep inside her.

"Don't worry, ma. I really like you and I'll be patient. I want you to enjoy me, not be afraid of me. But I'm telling you when you're ready I have a whole lot to give you," he said. Naseem brought her hand to his mouth and ran his tongue up her palm sensuously.

A bolt of pleasure shot straight from Katina's hand to between her legs. She saw in his eyes that he really wanted to give her what she never had. There was no doubt in her mind that he wanted to do her right then and there. He held off out of respect for her and his respect for her heightened hers for him.

Naseem was cool. A nigga who thought with his dick was destined to fail. What he planned to have with little mama was worth more than a nut. He took both of her hands in his and looked into her eyes. "We gonna wait to whenever you're ready," he said.

"Thank you," she replied feeling relieved that he still wanted her.

Naseem's dad told him once that if he ever came up on an innocent virgin who was totally smitten with him, she would give him the pussy with her mind, body, and soul. Naseem was not about to do anything that was going to get him kicked out of paradise.

CHAPTER 7

Listen to Your Heart

After Naseem dropped Katina at home, he was back in the streets hitting niggas off with work and trying to find the elusive witness he had been hunting. Antwan's murder was circulating and speculation on who had killed him ran rampantly. No one had connected Naseem's crew to Antwan's body so they were good but the person he really needed to see at the other end of his gun had yet to be revealed. Naseem made his runs checking his traps on Meeker and Pomona then he headed back to his apartment.

When he pulled up to his building he recognized Long's car sitting in the spot next to where he parked his BMW he pulled his truck into the empty spot next to Long and killed the engine. Long hoped out the car and they met at the rear of the vehicles.

"What's up, fam?" Naseem asked joining a hand with Long.

"Nothing much. Just checking the agenda for tomorrow," Long responded.

"I need to head over to see Baseem and drop off some

money and see what's up with the next shipment."

Naseem rested his foot up on the bumper of his truck.

"You want me to ride with you?"

"Nah, I got it. Plus I need you to try and see what's up with them niggas on Irvin Turner."

"Yeah, I heard Antwan's baby mother Stacy stay down there. You know, ain't no telling what that nigga told her," Long said bringing his arms up and folding them on his chest. "You want her dead or alive?"

Naseem stroked his chin trying to decide if he should have Long put down pleasure or pain. "Let her live for now we might be able to use that bitch to smoke out that rat."

Naseem decided to see what the business was before ordering her execution. If Stacy was the thirsty bitch he heard she was, then a few dollars might make her spill her guts.

"A'ight, you need anything else tonight?" asked Long.

"Nah, I'm about to get some rest. Chasing little mama around got a nigga on some high school shit," Naseem chuckled.

"You and little mama probably be on the phone, neither one of y'all want to get off be like you hang up first, no you. Like some little ass kids," Long teased with his hand up to his face like he was on a phone.

"Fuck you, nigga," Naseem spat but he couldn't get mad with the truth.

"I can't even front. I'm about to go snatch up Bre. She crazy as hell but sweet. I'm trying to feed her with a long spoon but she ready to bite a nigga hand."

"So, you been kicking it with Breonni?" Naseem smirked.

"Yeah, I trying to see what's behind all that slick tongue," Long remarked.

"You gonna get caught up," Naseem said putting his fist out ready to make his exit.

"You gonna already be there when I get there," Long cracked.

He touched fists with Naseem then turned to his car.

"Whatever, nigga," Naseem smirked. "Just don't have your face so deep in Bre's pussy that you forget about that business with Stacy."

"I'm on it, my nigga," Long assured him.

As Long pulled out the parking lot he began putting together a plan, he needed the right cheese to catch that rat bitch in his trap.

The next morning, Naseem placed a few calls, caught a little news and prepped to leave. Once he had all the money perfectly lined in the duffle bags he headed out the door. When he jumped in his ride he threw on Juelz Santana *Nobody Knows*. As he whipped down Central Avenue he eased the window down to feel the sun on his face. He pushed his whip as he watched the movement of the city singing along he cruised as the wind flowed through his car.

Nobody knows what I go through, nah. Nobody knows.
If you can put yourself inside my shoes, red bottoms.
You got friends is not friends no more, fuck em.
They don't understand this life that I chose.
Get money and when the money and fame, it can hurt everything you love.
That's right. I got some people that depend on me.

I can't give up, don't know what I'm going through.
You don't know, yeah, ah.

Naseem headed to Katina's house. He needed to take a quick ride over to New York and wanted to have her tight by his side. The sun was beaming through his window and his fresh cut and crisp white tee had his swag on ten. When he rolled up in front of her house he pulled out his cellphone and called inside.

Katina hurried out of her bathroom when she heard the ring tone she had programed just for Naseem. She dived across her bed and grabbed the phone from her bedside table.

"Hello," she answered slightly out of breath.

"What's up, ma? What you doing?"

"Hey, Naseem. Nothing much just washed my hair and about to chill. What you doing?" She turned on her back prepared to settle into the conversation.

"I'm in front of your house I want you to take a ride with me into the city."

Katina was quiet for a few seconds then she jumped up and went to the window to peek out.

"How long have you been out there?" she giggled and stepped back as if he could see her.

"Not long. Get dressed and come on."

"Okay. Give me ten minutes."

She disconnected the call and began to hurry through her room. She threw the towel off her head and brushed her hair into a neat bun. Then, she threw on a pair of blue jeans, a red t-shirt, and nice pair of three-inch open toe sandals. She brushed her teeth grabbed her clutch and hit the door.

"Where are you headed, young lady?" her mom asked, looking up from the newspaper.

"I'll be right back I'm just taking a quick ride. Love you," she answered her mom and ran out the door.

Her mother knew exactly what it was. She had seen some slight changes in her daughter that she knew only came with the attention of a man. She couldn't say much because Katina was still handling her business and appeared to be maintaining the morals she put in her. She smiled shook her head and went back to her reading.

When Naseem looked up from his call to Baseem, Katina was sashaying down the walkway. He hit the locks and reached over to open the door.

"Hey, baby," he said as she slid into her seat.

"Hey, yourself. You smell so good," she said. Katina smiled as she looked him over.

"And, you look so good. Can I kiss those pretty lips?" he asked leaning in to her.

Katina met him in the middle and gave him a few soft kisses on his lips. When she pulled back and saw her lip gloss she reached up and rubbed it in with her thumb. "I can't have you out here all glossy," she joked.

"I know, right? Can't be having niggas clowning."

Naseem licked his lips

"Where we going?" she asked.

"I have to go see my brother in the city."

"Oh, okay. Well, let's go. Can I hear some music?" she asked fastening her seat belt.

"You know I gotta pump the king on my way in the city."

He hit his CD changer and pulled up Jay Z's Blue Print.

"Oh shoot, play *A Dream*."

"You don't know nothing about that," he chuckled then he hit the track and pumped it.

"You better recognize," she said as she bopped slightly to the beat.

Naseem flashed her a smile as he pulled off headed to 280. They rocked and talked all the way to New York. Traffic was moving so they got right through the tunnel headed downtown. When he pulled into the pool hall parking lot Naseem turned down the music and called inside. Baseem instructed him to drive to the back of the parking lot and wait.

A few minutes later, Baseem and Chucky emerged from the back door puffing that loud.

Naseem looked over at Katina and said. "Let me handle this real quick. Just chill."

"Okay," she responded as Naseem exited the car. Her eyes focused on the tall brown skin man that looked just like Naseem. Katina decided that had to be his brother. His low cut and nicely trimmed goatee highlighted his features just right. The other guy was shorter with a smooth bald head and clear honey brown skin. Both men were dressed in dark jeans and black t-shirts.

Naseem popped the trunk and grabbed the duffle bag and headed in Baseem's direction.

"What's up?" Naseem asked, shaking his hand.

"You know how it is, upsetting the game and passing out condolences," Baseem spat then brought the blunt to his mouth.

"I hear that slick shit. What's up, Chuck?" he extended

is hand and gave him the coded shake.

"Sheeeiit. You know me. Hitting whatever this nigga miss," Chucky responded then reached out for the bag.

"So, is everything good over there?" Baseem asked passing Naseem the blunt.

Naseem took it to his mouth pulled deep then answered. "That bag is full not light so you know it's good for me but them niggas still on that bullshit. It's hot but I'm moving all around that shit. Hopefully, it will calm down in a few weeks."

"Them niggas still ain't learn. When you need the body to fall you gotta chop off the right heads," Baseem stated as he reached out for the blunt.

Naseem and Chucky nodded in agreement. "Who is that pretty young thing you got riding shot gun," Baseem asked as his eyes steeled on Katina.

"That's my baby girl," Naseem responded. He spotted the slight hunger in his brother's eyes.

"What they ran outta grown women over there in the Brick?" Baseem joked, bringing his gaze back to Naseem.

"Nah, I'm just tired of picking feathers to find out the bitch was a dog in disguise," Naseem shot back feeling a slight bit of attack.

"It's all good. Daddy always said get some untrained pussy and teach it your tricks," Baseem said and looked back at the car. "But a nigga like me I need my pony to know more than just one trick."

"I know that's right," Chucky chimed in. "Shit, I work too hard training theses niggas to act right. When I get come home I need to lay back and let the pussy make me know I'm the boss."

"I hear you. It's a good thing your mind don't work my dick," Naseem said, looking Chucky in the eye. Chucky was unwavering in his gaze as the two men exchanged a little heat.

Baseem looked back and forth between the two men and quickly ended the tension because neither wanted to back down.

"A'ight we'll catch you the next time. I'll be sending someone over with the next supply so you don't have to make the trip. Kayson said he will be ready to see you in a few weeks until then handle your business and keep your nose clean."

"I got you," Naseem said as he turned his attention to his brother.

They embraced and then pulled back. For the first time, the old feelings came rushing back strong. Naseem had done a great job at burying old bones but he could sense by Chucky's attitude that someone had been digging them up.

"See you next time," Chucky said extending his hand.

Naseem shook his hand but reminded himself to be cautious. He threw Chucky a smile but it was one that read more of watch your back rather than have a nice day.

When Naseem got to the car, his wheels began to turn. It wasn't his brother he would have to get out the way, it was his side kick. If Baseem and he bumped heads behind it, it would be a penalty he would be willing to pay.

Naseem headed back toward Jersey but could keep his mind off of the interaction he had with his brother and Chucky. Under normal circumstances, he would have laughed it off but with the history they shared he felt he had earned more respect.

"Why you so quiet?" Katina asked.

"Nothing. I'm just in deep thought." Naseem said as he forced himself to smile.

"You want to share?" she asked rubbing his arm.

Naseem thought for a few seconds then responded, "It's all good. I just haven't seen my brother in a while. Just trying to rebuild our bond."

He looked over at her and then back at the road.

"You wanna go get something to eat?"

"No, but I would like to show you something," she said with ease as she stared at the side of his face.

"Yeah, what you wanna show me?" he said with a flirtatious tone and sneaky grin.

Katina turned up her lips. "Not what you think."

She moved her hand up and down his arm.

"Take me to the overlook at Eagle Rock," she said then folded her hands on her lap.

Naseem looked over at her as he jumped on 280 West trying to catch her angle but she just kept her eyes forward. He was going to have to see what she wanted to show him when he got there.

Naseem parked the car, got out, and walked to her side to let her out. Katina took his hand and led him to the stone wall overlooking the city. Naseem stepped behind her and wrapped his strong arms around her waist. Katina rested her head back on his chest and breathed in the fresh air. There were trees of many colors and birds flying low. In the distance they could see down into the Valley of Jersey all the way over the tall buildings in New York. Even the air was different. There was peace that did not exist in the city. Up here, Katina felt free.

"You see that?" she asked as his eyes bounced over hundreds of trees.

"Yes, I do."

"You can have whatever you want in life if you just reach out and get it," she shared as she rested her hands on top of his.

Naseem looked out over the landscape as he took in her words. "I know but sometimes you have to take what is not given."

Katina heard the sigh leave his lips and knew that his mood was deeper than his words. She said, "Promise me something."

"What's that?"

"That you will heal the pain of the past."

Naseem kissed her neck. "I'm trying, baby girl," he said then focused his eyes back out into the distance.

"Just remember, you cannot enjoy your future if the past is a ball and chain around your ankle," she said as she squeezed his hands tight in hers.

Naseem just remained quiet. Her words carried more power than she knew. His main fear was that everything in his past would catch up to him and ruin all his plans for the future. If nothing else, he was determined to make sure that she was not harmed or tainted by what he had to do to make things right.

Naseem and Katina spent about an hour staring at the trees and talking before he dropped her off at home. Naseem went straight to Long to make him aware of his feelings about the meeting. It was time to strategize. They needed to erase some major players from the game.

CHAPTER 8

The Pact

"**D**amn, Raven, hurry up! I gotta go to the bathroom," Breonni said. She breathed down Raven's back as she fumbled around with her keys trying to open the door. "And, it's hot as hell out here. I'ma fuck around and pass out."

"Don't rush me. You should have went before we left school," she hurled back as the door popped open.

"Yo ass been living here for a hundred years and still don't know which key opens the door," Breonni mocked rolling her eyes as she brushed pass Raven rushing to the bathroom.

Raven sat her book bag at the bottom of the steps and picked up the pile of mail from the small table in the hallway. "Y'all can go in the den. I will be right there," she instructed Katina and Jovonna.

"You can go in the den all you want. I am going in the kitchen I'm hungry as hell," Jovanna said stepping out of her shoes and heading down the hallway. Katina wasted no time following right behind her.

"You are so greedy," Raven chuckled. She put down

the mail and followed her girls to the kitchen.

Jovanna went straight to the cabinet and pulled out the chips and a big bowl. Katina went to the other cabinet pulled out two bags of popcorn and hit the microwave.

"That's what the fuck I'm talking about," Breonni said as she bounced into the kitchen drying her hands on a paper towel.

"Don't be eating up all our food."

Raven gave her girls the stare down as she moved to the refrigerator and grabbed a bottle of Pepsi. She turned on the radio, danced over to the cabinets and grabbed a few glasses.

"Bitch, I am about to eat some of everything you got up in here and I'ma bite the cheese and put it back before I go," Breonni said. They all erupted in laughter.

"You so stupid," Raven laughed holding her stomach.

"Yup. I'll be stupid but I damn sure won't be hungry when I leave up out this soup kitchen," Breonni grabbed a bowl, a spoon, and a box of Apple Jack's. "Pass me the milk," she ordered as she hopped onto a stool.

Katina and Jovonna filled the bowl with chips and popcorn then sat on the stools next to Breonni. Raven threw some leftover chicken wings in the oven, poured everyone a tall glass of soda, and then posted up at the island.

"So what's up with you and Shawn?" she asked Jovonna.

All eyes went in her direction as they waited for her response. "I don't know we have to see," Jovanna said as she pulled her long wavy hair out the ponytail. She had a habit of slinging her hair like a white girl.

"Bitch, don't do that shit around the food," Breonni said covering her bowl.

"Shut up. My hair is clean."

"I don't give a fuck I don't want it in my mouth," Breonni said and wrinkled her brow.

"Whatever."

Jovonna grabbed her and kissed her hard on the cheek.

"Stop," Breonni said pulling away. "Now finish the story."

"There is nothing to really finish. He got my number from Katina and called me we talked for about thirty minutes then he asked me to hit the diner with him. He was cool but he kept making phone calls and that shit was a turn off."

"Well, you know them niggas are about that paper," Raven shot back as she moved to the oven to check the chicken.

"Yeah, I know and that's what scares me. Are we going to wait all this time, make all these sacrifices to graduate from high school, and keep our reputation clean and then become the girlfriends of some block niggas? I don't know." Jovonna sighed and reached for her glass.

"Look, I know we made oaths and promises but you can't help who you fall in love with," Katina said grabbing a handful of chips.

"Bitch, what that nigga over there saying to yo ass at night?" Breonni said. She checked Katina's forehead for fever.

"Nothing that Long ain't saying to you," Katina responded with her lips twisted to the side.

"Well, excuse me, Ms. Naseem!" Breonni turned her attention back to her cereal.

"I'm just saying let's give them a chance and see what

happens," Katina added.

"You really like Naseem, huh?" Raven asked, grabbing a few paper plates from the top of the refrigerator.

"Yes, I do. He is very respectful and he listens to me," Katina said looking Raven in the eyes.

"I hear that. Well, do you, ma," Raven said supportively.

"Whatever. So, did you go out with Flint the other night, Rav?" Breonni put the ball in Raven's court.

"No, but he took me to breakfast the next morning and he was high as hell, fucking that food up. I was so nervous sitting across from him I couldn't even eat my food. My stomach was messed up."

"Bitch, stop being scary," Breonni said, pouring another bowl. "You only live once I am not spending my life being afraid to have a good time."

"We know you be with Long more than his personal thoughts," Jovanna chimed in.

"Don't hate." Breonni flagged her hand bringing her spoon to her mouth.

"But on the real we gotta be careful. It's good to have a nice time but if you are too fucked up to realize it then it all was for nothing," Jovanna continued.

"What you mean, JoJo?" Katina softly asked.

"We don't know shit about these niggas. They are used to dealing with chics that are in that life. We have never had sex or been in love. If we step off into the big league we can get hurt real bad, real fast. I just don't want to have any regrets."

She looked at each one of her girls. Each of them stopped to think about what Jovonna had said. Katina looked down at her hands. She knew Jovonna's words were true but her attraction to Naseem was way too strong to let him go. Everything about him turned her on. His eyes, his lips, the way he touched her and every word that fell from his mouth made her want to give him everything she had. She was not about to turn back now.

"Well, let's just be careful. And, promise to always lean on each other."

Katina lifted her head and connected eyes with Raven.

Raven nodded her understanding. She knew that Katina was her rock and all that she had been through over the years Katina was her strength and the only one to hold her darkest secrets.

"Yeah, Yeah, Yeah. Y'all bitches getting me depressed up in here," Breonni joked, trying to lighten the mood.

"You would mess up a wet dream," Raven added with a chuckled.

"I *am* the reason for wet dreams. You better ask some-body," Breonni teased and did a little dance on her stool.

Katina nudged her with her elbow. Even though Breonni was loud and open Katina knew better than anybody else that Bre was a scared little girl on the inside. She was just praying that her girl didn't get into something she could not talk or joke her way out of.

"Well, I think I might just wait until I get to college and see what them Gamma boys talkin' about," Jovonna said and slapped hands with Raven.

"Girl, go ahead and fuck around with them Gamma boys if you want to. You gonna be drunk as hell with a train behind you."

"That's nasty."

Jovonna scrunched her face at the thought.

"Yeah, I know. Have yo ass up in class the next day with your pussy sitting next to you doing a line up."

"A line up?" Katina asked with curiosity.

"Yeah, she'll be like was that him? How about him? Pussy be all confused. Don't do it, JoJo," Breonni pleaded putting her arm around her shoulder.

They all burst into laughter.

"You crazy as hell," Raven managed to say between screaming laughter.

They continued to laugh, talk and eat as they rocked to the variety of music that played on the radio.

"Why y'all making all this gotdamn noise in my house?" a deep voice boomed from behind them.

Raven instantly came to attention and looked in her father's direction. The smiles fell from Jovonna and Katina's face. Breonni continued to eat her food as she responded. "What's up Pops? We just chillin'."

"Why y'all ain't chillin' at yo house eating shit up?" he moved into the kitchen looking each girl over.

"Because your food taste better and you are so hospitable," Breonni joked. She was the only one who played with him.

"I got yo hospitable," he spat back with his wicked grin.

"I bet you do," she mumbled looking at his well-maintained body. Even though he was sick and not the man he was just a few years ago he was still fine as hell.

"Raven, hurry up with your friends. I got something I need you to do." he said looking her in the eyes.

"Yes, Daddy," she responded as she began to clean up the mess they had made.

All of the laughter had been sucked out of the room. Breonni looked back and forth at Raven and her father and became uncomfortable. Katina just looked down. Jovonna formed a wrinkle in her brow. They all hated the fact that Raven would always be stuck in the house and to make matters worse her father never appreciated anything she accomplished. All he did was nag and complain.

"Where is my chicken at?" Breonni asked to break up the monotony.

Raven took a deep breath swallowed her spit then grabbed the pot holders.

"Pops, why you always messing with my girl?" Breonni asked.

"Hurry up and eat so you can leave. You making my house hot," he jabbed back again smiling at her like she was on the menu. He then looked over at Jovonna allowing his eyes to travel up her legs and rest on her thigh.

Jovanna tried to keep her eyes forward. As she could feel his hot gaze that felt like a hundred filthy hands slithering all over her body.

"Whatever. Wrap mines to go," Breonni hopped off the stool and took her bowl to the sink.

Glen watched the way her short skirt sway as she moved. Breonni paid his flirtatious attitude no mind. She put away the cereal and grabbed the foil to wrap up her chicken.

"Hurry up, Raven," he said as he exited the kitchen. "And, I don't want to see y'all little faces for at least a week."

"We love you, too," Breonni yelled as he walked down the hallway.

Jovonna shook her head. She could not stand his ass. Ever since Raven's mother left, Raven had to be the cook and the maid. He was like an evil task master always barking orders and talking to her like she was the dirt from the bottom of his shoe.

Raven wrapped the chicken as she fought back tears. When she turned to her girls she forced a smile and whispered, "Here. Now go ahead so I can help my dad. I might be able to sneak out after he falls asleep."

"Bitch, you are not going to have a problem keeping your virginity because the number one cock blocker is on your team," Breonni joked, hugged her tightly, and continued, "If you can get out, call me. Me and Long will pick you up."

"Call me tonight," Katina echoed as she looked at her friend feeling her turmoil.

"I will," Raven promised. She gave her a big smile that said I love you and thank you at the same time. Katina smiled back but inside she cried for her.

"Come on before he fuck up my good mood," Breonni said as she headed to the door. Katina and Jovonna followed close behind.

Raven was living in hell. They hoped that one day she would be free but the scars of her father's treatment would always imprison her spirit.

CHAPTER 9

She's Young but She's Ready

"Good Morning, princess," Katina's mom announced as she drew back her curtains.

Katina picked up her head and peaked at her mom through the slits of her eyes then laid her head back on the pillow.

"Mom why are you so loud?" she whined.

"Get up. You have to be ready for your solo. I have breakfast waiting and Raven should be here shortly. Let's go, Beloved."

Her mom patted her leg as she headed out the room. Katina stretched, threw back her covers and headed to the bathroom. As she was brushing her teeth her phone rang. She moved to answer and the voice that made her tingle came through the speaker.

"Good morning, babe," Naseem's half asleep growl boomed in her ear.

"Good morning, Nas," she cooed as she took a seat on the edge of the bed.

"I just wanted to wish you luck. Do your best and play

from your heart," he encouraged as he turned over on his back.

"Thank you. I will play with you on my mind," she blushed as the words left her lips.

"That's what's up. Make me proud and hit me when you get done."

"I will."

"Give me a kiss," he said.

Katina wasted no time giving him a big kiss through the phone as she giggled and covered her face.

"That will hold me, talk to you later," he responded. Her shy giggle warmed his heart.

"Okay, get some rest."

When they disconnected the call she threw on her robe and headed downstairs smiling ear to ear.

"I guess that little boy must have called you," her mom said looking up from the toaster.

"Maybe," Katina replied as she took a seat at the table.

Her mom smiled and began preparing her plate. As Katina reached for the newspaper the doorbell rang.

"I'll get it."

Katina took off toward the door.

When she opened the door, she knew immediately that Raven was distraught. She took her by the hand and pulled her inside.

"I can't do this much longer," Raven confessed as Katina pulled her to the dining room.

"Did it happen again?" Katina whispered.

Raven nodded her head as tears welled up in her eyes. Katina grabbed her into her arms and hugged her tightly.

"You gotta get out, Rav," she said as she squeezed tighter.

"I can't," Raven responded in a shaky voice.

"Don't worry. A way will be created soon. I love you, Rav."

Katina, too, began to cry. Raven settled into Katina's embrace like a small child. She was her peace and salvation. Katina gave her a few more seconds to release some of her agony then she wiped her face and let her go.

"Come here. Let me play something for you."

Raven lifted her head and followed Katina to the piano. They both took a seat on the bench then Katina slid back the shiny black shield to reveal the keys.

Taking a deep breath, Katina slowly began to tickle the ivory. Each stroke of the keys was like a warm hug. Raven put her head down on Katina's lap and listened to the comforting sounds that were more than music to her ears. Katina was the only one in the world that held her secret and shared her pain. Raven knew that she needed to get out but fear and guilt made her stay.

Katina's mom stood in the doorway and silently watched as her daughter helped build a shield around Raven's heart. The tender, yet strong, tone of the piano touched her soul. She placed her hand on her chest and closed her eyes. Her daughter's hands had the gift of healing. After enjoying a few minutes of the melody, she headed back to the kitchen allowing the girls to have their moment. Still, deep inside she knew that there was a pain that plagued Raven that needed to be revealed and erased forever.

Katina played. She didn't speak another word. She already had decided that when she was more comfortable with Naseem she was going to tell him everything. Then, she would ask him for an unthinkable favor.

* * * * *

Until now, Naseem had been just marinating the pussy. This weekend he was planning on lighting that pussy on fire.

"Yo, ma, I brought you something real nice. I'm going to bring it to you at our spot. I want you to wear it this weekend when we go out," he said into the phone as he cruised down the parkway.

"Awww. You are so good to me," Katina beamed.

"You deserve it. Did you pass that test?"

"Yes. I got an A."

"That's a good girl. Daddy is going to have to give you a special treat."

"I hope so." Katina smiled as the thoughts of how his hands roamed over her body.

"I'll catch y'all later," Katina said to her girls while tucking her phone in her purse.

"Damn, all that nigga gotta do is say go and this bitch run a marathon," Breonni announced stopping to stare at her sideways.

"I love you too," she sang as she crossed the street headed to the playground.

"We love you, too, Tina," Jovonna yelled back.

"Stop hating," she said to Breonni and they continued to walk home from school.

Breonni didn't even respond. She adjusted her purse on her shoulder and kept it moving.

When Naseem pulled up to the side of Colgate Park, Katina hopped in his car wearing a big smile on her face.

"Why you all cheesed up?" he asked giving back the

same energy she was giving him.

"I'm happy to see you. Is that a crime?"

"I guess not," Naseem said leaning forward to get his kiss.

Katina put her hand behind his head pulling him towards her. When his tongue entered her mouth she tilted her head and received all he had to offer.

"It feels like you more than miss me," he said as she released his head.

Katina licked her lips as her heart rate picked up. A sexy smile came over her face then she covered her mouth and giggled.

"Don't get shy now," he said as he pulled away from the curb.

Naseem headed towards her house to drop her off before he went to meet Long.

"Call me when you come in tonight," Katina said as she reached into her book bag.

"Okay," Naseem agreed. He reached into the back seat to grab some gifts he had picked up for her but he was not the only one who had a surprise today.

Katina had a small box in her hands. She held it out to him and smiled from ear to ear.

"What's that?" he asked with curiosity all over his face.

"Open it," she said and pushed the box toward him.

Naseem gave her the bags then opened the box. When his eyes settled on what was inside, he looked up at her. Katina flashed him a shy grin.

"Put it on," she said as she helped him remove it from the small jewelry box. The gold Bulova watch fit his wrist just right.

"This was a grip. Let me find out you been stealing out of mommy's purse," he joked knowing she didn't have a job and no money coming in.

"Ha ha, very funny. You are always giving me money so I just saved up and got you something I knew you didn't have."

Naseem was impressed.

"That's what's up. You sweet as hell. Give me a kiss before you end up giving me something else I never had before."

"Oh, Lord," she said and leaned in and kissed him. "Talk to you later."

She got out and headed into the house.

Katina was scared but, at the same time, she had been waiting for Naseem to make another move. Every Friday and Saturday when they got together he would say all kinds of nasty things to her. He kissed and touched her in ways that she never thought could feel so good but, at the end of the night, he always took her home leaving the agreement between them intact. However, this Friday would be the Friday of all Fridays.

* * * * *

The week had flown by. Katina's solo was out the way. School was almost over and things between Naseem and her were moving faster than they both expected. Friday night, they pulled up to Benihana in Short Hills and walked inside. They joked and talked as they waited to be seated.

Katina looked delectable in the black Versace dress and

pumps Naseem had bought her. Her body was scented from head to toe and her legs were shining and fabulous extending from her dress.

"I have never been here before," she said excitedly as the chief stepped to the grill and started their meal.

"This shit is on point," Naseem said. His taste buds began to do a dance on his tongue. He flagged the waitress and ordered a drink while the cook laid out the meat and vegetables on the grill.

Katina looked on as the Asian gentleman did tricks with the utensils and seasonings. She even clapped a few times.

Naseem felt good watching her enjoy the night. He put his arm around her whispering in her ear. Katina's face turned beet red as he gave her a few highlights of what he wanted later.

"You are so nasty," she shyly stated.

Naseem just gave her a sneaky smile then took a sip of his Sake.

Their plates were placed in front of them and they began to dig in. Katina closed her eyes and enjoyed the different flavors that exploded in her mouth.

Naseem enjoyed watching her all night. She was watching him, too, hoping that she was going to get to do more of those big girl things.

As the meal came to an end, Katina took several nervous trips to the bathroom. Every time she walked past a mirror she twirled and giggled thinking, *I look like good as hell.*

She plopped down in her seat and grabbed her purse.

"You ready to go, ma?" Naseem pulled out some

money and dropped it on the table.

"Yes, I am."

"Can Daddy have a kiss?" Naseem didn't wait for a response instead he leaned in and kissed Katina like she was the air he needed to breath. He slid his hand up her inner-thigh, rubbing up and down her leg. It caught her so off guard that she clamped her legs on his hand and slid back. Naseem laughed.

"Damn, if you scared get a dog. Who's responsible for that security system? ADT?"

Katina giggled displaying an innocent smile to cover her embarrassment.

"You so bad," she said looking at the sly grin on his face.

"I am," he admitted, "but lucky for you I stopped."

"To be honest, I didn't want you to. I'm more than ready."

Her sudden bold statement caused Naseem to stand up in more ways than one.

As they got up to leave, all Naseem could think was, *Yeah, I'm going to loosen that ass up tonight.*

Back at his place Katina was walking around on that soft ass carpet thinking about how tonight was going to change her whole world. Naseem put on some music, dimmed the lights, lit a few candles around the living room, and set up the items he needed for a night of pleasure.

Tonight he would be able to do all the things he had planned and could take his time. Katina's parents were out of town and he didn't have to rush to get her home.

"You want to dance?" Naseem asked walking over to

her and extending his hand.

"Yes, I do," she responded as she reached out to him.

Naseem took her hand, kissed it, and then pulled her close to him as he sang along with Keith Sweat.

You may be young but you're ready, ready to learn,
you're not a little girl, you're a woman, take my hand,
let me tell you, baby.

Katina was relaxed as she moved slowly in Naseem's arms. He began to rub up and down her back kissing and sucking on her neck. He slid her dress off of her shoulder and sucked gently on her collar bone before nibbling on her breast. Katina was in a zone. The soft music and his warm lips on her skin set her body aflame.

When Naseem looked up and saw all the submission written on her face he knew it was time to turn her out.

"I have a surprise for you. Come in the kitchen." He said as he led her there.

Katina walked on wobbly legs as her heart skipped beats of anticipation.

Naseem had a towel on the counter and a squeeze bottle of honey. Right in front of it was a stool. He lifted Katina by the waist and sat her up on the counter. "Daddy needs a little dessert," he said seductively.

"I guess I have something to do with that," Katina replied. She was open to whatever he had planned.

"Damned right you do," he responded with hunger in his eyes.

"Well, what are you going to have?"

"Something hot, wet, and sticky."

Oh, my god, what did that mean? What was the honey for and where was he going to put it? She thought as he guided her dress above her waist.

Keith crooned *I want to go outside in the rain*. The mood was just right because Naseem was about to make her pussy flood.

Naseem pulled the stool up to the edge of the counter and sat eye level with the pussy. He slid his hand up her thigh sending chills all through her body. Katina looked down at him as her body began moving to the touch of his hands.

"I want you to relax and let me make my pussy talk," he uttered as he grabbed the bottle of honey and started to pour it up and down her inner thigh.

Katina looked on in amazement. She gasped deeply as the cool honey drizzled onto her skin. Gripping the edge of the counter she tried to prepare herself for what was going to happen next. But with no prior sexual experience she couldn't even imagine the type of pleasure she was in for. After he had her nice and sticky he cupped his arms under her legs and slid her to the edge of the counter. Naseem slid the tip of his tongue along her leg then licked and sucked her inner thigh.

Katina's breathing got heavy as she rubbed the top of Naseem's head. He lapped at the crease in the inside of her upper thigh then kissed her pussy through her panties. Katina arched her back and held on to the end of the counter as the sensations rose from her toes to the top of her head.

Once Naseem saw that he had her body totally under his command he reached up and slowly pulled her panties down allowing the tips of his fingers to firmly caress her thighs.

Naseem stared at her perfect flower then kissed it gently. He then grabbed the honey and poured it on her clit and watched it run down her lips. When it dripped all the way down, he caught it with his tongue and licked all the way up.

Katina watched his calculated actions as her body jerked with every touch of his tongue. Instinctively, she tried to close her legs but couldn't because he had them held firmly open with his strong grip. Naseem zoomed in and attacked, placing his warm mouth onto her clit.

"Ooohhh," Katina moaned loudly grabbing the back of his head.

Naseem went to work, licking and sucking. Katina rested her head against the cabinet and gyrated her hips. She had no idea where those moves were coming from. They seemed second-nature.

"Ssss," she hissed, "wait."

She tried to slow down his movements but Naseem ignored her command.

"I have to pee. Wait Naseem…"

Naseem just kept taking her higher. She pushed her head harder into the cabinet door and wiggled in his arms as he lit her whole body on fire.

"Aaahh—ahhhh," she moaned out as her breathing quickened.

Naseem had her whole clit in his mouth sucking it like a sweet candy drop and he was ready to receive all her nectar.

Katina's legs started to shake uncontrollably and she went from moaning to yelling out his name.

"Nas—Nas," she started to cry and skeet at the same

time.

Naseem kept on going. He knew that he had to get her open to him so he could have her totally with no resistance. He made her come again and again until she couldn't take it anymore. He knew she reached her peak when she wasn't able to speak or open her eyes.

He stood up and flashed a sexy smile. He reached for the other towel to wipe his face then proceeded to tenderly slide two fingers into her. Naseem wanted to get her ready for all those inches he was packing. The pussy was tight as hell gripping his fingers snug between her walls as he felt for her spot. Katina moaned, grabbed Naseem around his neck, and bit into his shoulder as he picked up the pace.

"That feels good," Katina moaned.

"What? This right here?" Naseem asked with confidence knowing he had that spot.

Katina started to moan out in ecstasy once again. "Oooohhhh—yes—yes," she was squeezing him for dear life.

Naseem had found her spot and was not going to let it go. He slid one more finger inside her and started to move a little faster. She moved in sync with his fingers to make sure he could stay right in that spot.

"Look at you, ma. You like what Daddy is doing to that pussy, don't you?" he breathed heavily in her ear.

"Yeeeees—Yeeees," she cried out as an orgasm snuck up on her.

Naseem allowed her to ride the wave until it subsided. Then he took her to the peak once again. This time when she spilled her honey she was left spent. Her arms draped over his shoulders as she rested her forehead on his chest trying to stop her head from spinning.

It's time, was all that Naseem could think. He picked her up off of the counter and carried her to his room. He laid her back on his bed and admired her perfect curves.

Katina knew she was at the point of no return. Naseem climbed between her legs and began placing soft wet kisses on her neck and shoulders. He eased her dress over her head and threw it to the floor. He looked down at her sleepy glow, then took one of her breast out of her bra and started to suckle softly. Katina felt as if the room was spinning.

Naseem stopped to take off his shirt and open his pants. He kissed and sucked her lips then he bit into her neck. His dick hardened at the thought of how good she was going to feel.

He paused and whispered into her ear, "You alright? You want me to stop?"

"No, don't stop," she lowered her voice and eyes.

Naseem stood up and pulled his jeans and boxers all the way down then slid on a Magnum. He could hear *Make it Last Forever* coming from the radio and he was going to do just that. Climbing back on top of Katina, he gently kissed and licked everything he could get his mouth on.

Katina was on fire and in complete submission. Her pussy was soaking wet as Naseem began to slide in one inch at a time. "Ssssss—oooohh."

"You alright?"

"Yes."

Katina squeezed her eyes real tight.

"Baby, please, be gentle," she whispered.

"Relax—mmmmm—just relax," he advised when he

felt her body tense up.

Naseem kept repeating it softly in her ear as he continued to get her fit to his size. He could tell he was hurting her because she was scratching the hell out of him but he wasn't trying to stop. Once he was fully inside, he stayed there and enjoyed the tightness. He wanted to give her a chance to recover before he started to handle the pussy.

Naseem started to stroke in and out slowly causing Katina to moan and breathe loudly.

"You want me to stop?" he asked with concern.

"No, please don't stop," she panted.

"Okay, baby, I got you," he answered not even missing a stroke.

"Nas. Nas. Nas." she called his name repeatedly.

"Yes, baby," he moaned in her ear.

"I love you."

Her admission gave him a since of achievement and caused him to pick up a little speed.

Naseem started to moan himself.

"Mmmm—damn—you feel good," he whispered into her ear. He hadn't had tight pussy like that in years.

"I love you too," he heard himself say.

Naseem put one of her legs on his shoulder and dipped slowly in and out of her wetness causing her body to surrender to his demands.

Katina began to cum again. Her pain turned into pleasure as he continuously hit her spot.

Naseem released her leg and pushed himself deep inside her and kissed her passionately as he grinded against her clit sending sensations of ecstasy through her whole body.

That virgin pussy was getting a complete lesson tonight. Katina held on tight and Naseem kept going. Katina just went with the flow as he took her from one position to another.

For the rest of the night Naseem sucked, licked and sexed Katina into a coma. She was beyond satisfied. She couldn't even move.

Naseem eased off the bed headed to the bathroom. Upon his return he just stood and admired his handiwork. The sheets half covered her naked body and she looked like an angel sound asleep. He crawled up next to her and fell asleep as well.

The next morning Katina and Naseem awoke and took a shower together. She could not believe that she had just got eaten out, had sex and multiple orgasms and was now in the shower with a grown ass man. Her pussy was sore as hell but she wanted him to do it all over again. She had heard how the first time could be so terrible but with the feelings she had for him put her body at ease. He made it more than a night to remember.

Naseem was in a daze as he stared at her perfect body. *Damn, I'm in love with a young girl. What part of the game is this?* He wondered with a smile across his face.

"Why you smiling?" Katina asked, breaking his train of thought.

"Thinking about how those pretty legs was shaking on my shoulders."

"Is that a good thing?" She moved a little closer to him as the water cascaded over their bodies.

"Hell, yeah. You made me put in some work."

"Well, you started it." she blushed.

Naseem wrapped his arms around her. He was ready to go again. "Come mere let finish what I started. You good with that?" he asked.

"Yup, if Daddy is going to kiss it and make it better first."

Katina was wide open now and couldn't wait to feel the way he made her feel on that counter.

"I got you ma." Naseem went down to his knees and put one of her legs on his shoulder and went to work.

Katina was in heaven and Naseem was now her god.

CHAPTER 10

Breonni

Breonni had also been out on several dates with Long but he had not put any moves on her. It was more like they were best friends than a couple. Every day after school, Long picked her up and took her with him on all his runs. She would sit pretty in the front seat and make all the bitches jealous. A few times a couple females confronted him about having her in the car and he checked their asses immediately; however, he never took their relationship to the next level. Bre was getting ready to change all that.

"What's up, my nigga?" Sussex Ave said to Long as he got out the car.

Breonni sat watching their transaction. After a few minutes of intense conversation Sussex bent two fingers in his mouth and whistled, causing three other guys to emerge from a nearby alley. They approached with mean looks on their faces as they joined in on the conversation. A minute or so later they returned from the alley with bulging prints under their shirts.

Long opened the door and let Breonni out and put her in the back then climbed in after her. Sussex jumped in the driver's seat and one of the other guys jumped in the passenger seat.

When Breonni looked around she saw that the other two were in a car parked across the street and took off as Sussex took off right behind them. The two cars moved through the streets with precision and after about twenty minutes they were pulling up to Georgia King Village. The men hopped out of the cars and moved towards the buildings. Sussex came to the window and said a few words to Long then went in the same direction as the other men.

"Is everything alright?" Bre asked.

"Yeah, it's all good." he said smoothly as he slid down in his seat, pulled a blunt out his pocket and lit it up.

Long sat puffing and watching the area.

Breonni was bored. She sat sucking on a lollipop and sighing every so often in between the music that was softly coming from the speakers. The area had gotten dark and the only activity was a few crack heads moving back and forth and the dudes who were servicing them. Breonni sat there evaluating her relationship with Long. She realized that there would be no movement if she didn't initiate it.

Breonni threw her lollipop stick out of the window. She reached over and unzipped Long's jeans and slid her hand in the slit of his boxers. Long kept his eyes focused on the buildings as Breonni began doing her thing. After a few seconds of stroking him firmly in her hand his dick was at full attention. She leaned in and ran her tongue around the rim of his dick then placed the head in her mouth and did it like her lollipop. When her jaws tightened around the head he looked down as a slight hiss left his lips. Breonni rotated from soft gentle sucks to firmer ones then took him to the back of her throat.

"Damn, ma." he said as he looked down and watched her handle that pole like a professional.

Long watched on in amazement. Shorty was official. He wanted to lean his head back and enjoy but he had to divide his attention between Breonni and his mission at hand. Just as he was about to release, his phone rang.

"Speak," he said into the receiver. After a brief pause he said, "A'ight, come on."

Long hung up then put all his attention on Breonni as he began to release what felt like buckets.

Breonni continued to take him in deep, swallowing every drop. She rose up slowly releasing him from her jaw grip. She placed the steel back in his pants and zipped him up. Grabbing another lollipop from her purse, she removed the wrapper and placed it into her mouth. Breonni tightened her jaws on the lollipop and looked into Long's eyes. Long looked at her and gave her a cocky smile.

"I was about to tell you to stop sucking them lollipops but, as you can see, a nigga done had a change of heart."

"You better stop sleeping on a bitch and step your game up," she said as she sat back in her seat.

"I got you, ma," he said as his boys climbed back into the car breathing hard and pulling off fast.

Bre looked at the guy in the passenger seat and noticed blood on his shirt and hands. At that moment she realized she was definitely involved with some killers. She smiled and savored the thought.

CHAPTER 11

'Cause I Said So

Long moved around his house preparing himself for the night at hand. He knew that shit was about to pop off so he had to be ready for the fall out. They put fear in them niggas last night so it was only a matter of time before they would try and strike back. He walked into his kitchen and grabbed a bottle of Patron and a few glasses and set them on the coffee table. He rolled and lit a blunt, sat back and crossed his feet at the ankles. He wanted to be relaxed when his crew got there, but just as he was getting into his comfort zone he heard a few hard knocks at the door. Long set the blunt in the ashtray and moved towards the door.

One by one his boys filed in, all except Shawn. Long moved back to his seat and looked around the room at the faces of his most loyal comrades. Having a thorough team was more important than having a gun full of bullets in the middle of a shootout. Shit, you might hit a target or you might not but he knew for certain that, if shit jumped off, each one of the men in that room would lay a nigga down and sell his body parts to his mama at his funeral—buy one, get one free.

"So, what's good, my niggas?" Long asked as he began filling the glasses to the top.

"You already know we trying to take it to the next level," Naseem said reaching for his glass. "I think we are in a very good position to take over the whole fucking city."

He grabbed the blunt from the ashtray and lit up.

Flint thought for a minute. He lifted his drink, took a shot to the head, slammed his glass down on the table, and then nodded for another one.

"We gotta work smart not hard. With them niggas warring, we can come from every angle and set up shop. We gotta make sure we keep this circle tight and move like we don't trust no fucking body," Flint said. As he spoke, his face balled up like the words had a nasty taste to them.

Naseem nodded in agreement. What Flint had said was real spit.

"You already know if I ain't starve with you, I ain't eating with you," Naseem added.

Taking a swig of gin, he cleared his throat and wiped his mouth with the sleeve of his shirt. "So what is the status from last night?" he asked then sat back and waited for the report.

"I sent Sussex and his boys up in there," Long reported then took a drink to the head. "They got them niggas to give up some information but not enough. I know where Antwan's shorty lives. She moved to Bakery Village on 4th Ave. I'ma pay her a visit in a couple days."

"A'ight. Well, handle your business and keep me informed," Naseem spat.

He reached over and grabbed the blunt and lit it up again.

"Where the fuck is Shawn ass at?" he asked looking around the room.

"Man, that nigga held up in some pussy. I would have smacked the shit out of him a long time ago if it wasn't for Nas," Flint said.

"Is he with Katina's girl Jovonna?" Naseem asked.

"Nah, he with that scandalous ass Robin. I can't stand that bitch," Long's mouth felt sick just mentioning her name. For some reason, Shawn loved that bitch. He had been fucking with her since eighth grade but that bitch was on every nigga in the hood's resume. No matter how much time would pass, she would always find her way back in Shawn's bed and his pocket.

"Nigga fucking up, Nas," Flint said shaking his head.

"You know I promised his brother I would not let that nigga fall but he gonna make me take my words back from a dying man's ears," Naseem put his glass down and took a deep breath. "Get that nigga on the phone."

Flint dialed the number and put the phone on speaker.

"Hello," Shawn answered groggily.

As soon as he heard Shawn's voice Long sprung up from his seat ready to go in. Naseem put his hand up to stop him.

"Nigga, where the fuck you at?" Naseem barked before Long could part his lips.

"I'm chillin', what's up?" Shawn replied with a nonchalance that infuriated Long.

"Muthafucka, can you tell time?" Long snapped.

"Oh, shit, my bad. I didn't think y'all really needed me," he stated lamely. A female could clearly be heard in the background.

Long took a deep breath to stop himself from trying to climb through the phone. Gritting his teeth he said to Naseem, "Is this nigga crazy?"

"Yeah, and stupid, too," replied Naseem.

"Yo, my nigga, I think you better get right and get yo ass over here," Flint broke in.

"Damn, I'm kinda tied up. Can't y'all just fill a nigga in? You know how it is," he stated right before a slight hiss slipped from his lips.

"This nigga fucking while he talking to us?" Flint asked looking over at Long.

Long ran his hands over his face. "That's yo boy," he said to Naseem.

Naseem was ready to go ham.

"Yo, my nigga, get the fuck up. Put that bitch on the fucking bus and get yo ass over here immediately," he ordered without raising his voice.

"Damn, a'ight. You want me to just do her like that? What am I supposed to say?"

"Tell that bitch 'cause I fucking said so, muthafucka!" Naseem stood up, snatched the phone and hit the end button. He couldn't listen to another word that came out that nigga mouth or he was going to kill him on sight.

"This nigga," he shook his head. "Man, pour me something else before I blow the fuck up."

"Yo boy is incompetent," Long stated.

"Nah, that nigga pussy whipped," Flint blurted raising the blunt to his lips.

"How the fuck do a nigga get that shit?" Long asked, looking puzzled.

"Get what shit?" Flint laughed.

"Whipped. That shit don't even sound right. Damn nigga. Get in that shit, lay a bitch down and pull the fuck out. How hard is that?" He shook his head.

"Man, you would be amazed. The tricks these bitches be doing with their jaws and walls," Flint said then chuckled again.

Naseem looked over at him and had to laugh, himself. "Did that nigga say jaws and walls?"

Long smiled, "Sheeeiit. If that bitch ain't got an ass full of cash I can't see it."

"Man, you crazy as hell," Flint said taking a drink.

"A'ight let's get back to business before his ass gets here. He ain't in on this new shit. I just wanted to make him come all the way over to this muthafucka."

Naseem took a seat and finished mapping out the plan. He gave each man his role and each agreed. When the next move was etched in stone they held their glasses up and toasted to their success.

Long felt the hot liquor hit the back of his throat. He wondered if Shawn would get right or if he would have to do some explaining to Naseem. He sure wasn't going to let that nigga fuck up what they were building. With an eye witness still unidentified, the last thing they needed was to have a bitch nigga on the team. Shawn had made it a habit of dropping the ball. His absence the night they killed Antwan had Long thinking that the nigga was afraid to get blood on his hands. It was Long's motto that is a nigga won't get dirty with you, he might do dirt to you. He had no intention of finding out the hard way. Long planned to keep that nigga, Shawn, as far away from his business as possible.

CHAPTER 12

On the Block

"Come on, Bre. Damn!" Raven yelled through the bathroom door as anxiety kicked in.

"Calm yo ass down, that nigga ain't going nowhere." Breonni came out the bathroom fixing her pants. She looked at Raven and wrinkled her brow.

"Whatever. You taking all long. They gonna bounce."

"This bitch," Breonni said, shaking her head as she moved to put on her sneakers.

"Rav, they be out there all the time. Where are they going?" Jovonna asked as she flipped through a black hair magazine. "Oh, and I thought you wasn't feeling him like that."

"Yeah, I was ready to cancel that nigga contract until he let me push that whip a few days ago. Bitches was looking. I had the window down hair blowing in the wind," she chuckled.

"You know this bitch need medication, all excited 'cause she got enough hair to blow in the damn wind," Breonni joined in.

"Shut up, you be all on Long dick, too."

"Whatever. Let me blow something real quick," Breonni asked trying to go for her weed.

"No, come on. Flint told me to be out there at five o'clock and I don't want to miss him."

"I hope that nigga give you what you need so you can relax 'cause you getting on my damn nerves. Move—" She nudged her to the side and grabbed her money off of the dresser.

"Come on," she said shooting Raven a dirty look.

"I love you, too, Bre."

Breonni, Jovonna, and Raven hopped in the cab and headed down to Pomona Avenue in the Weequaic section. When they pulled up, the block was knocking. Flint was posted up against his car talking on his cell phone. When he looked up and saw the three of them, he disconnected the call and waved them across the street.

Raven had a bright smile plastered across her face. She was in her glory. He had sent for her and she was drooling as she got closer and her eyes began to take in all his features. The sun had put a nice tint to his mocha skin. Her eyes roamed from his feet to the top of his head where his low brushed waves had her ready to dive in.

"Why you looking at me like that, little mama?" Flint asked, snapping her out of her fantasy.

"A'int nobody looking at you," she shot back.

"You ain't scared to talk shit, huh?" he asked giving her a sexy smirk.

"I don't scare easily," she responded.

"We will see about that," he said, looking her up and down. He was well pleased with all the curves that stared back at him. "Yeah, I got some plans for you."

"I am counting on it," she continued to flirt with him.

"We gonna bounce in a minute. Y'all get in my car."

He handed Raven the keys.

Raven took the key from his hand rubbing her fingers over his hand. A tickle formed in her belly and chill bumps rose on her arm as she moved to the car.

"You don't have to sneak and touch me. If you want to touch me all you gotta do is say, 'let me get some of that'."

"Can I get some of that?" she asked and pouted her plump lips.

Flint took her by her hand and pulled her into his arms. Raven put her arms around his back and, as her breast rested against his chest, his hands caressed the small of her back pulling her in even closer. She closed her eyes briefly and allowed his scent to enhance all her senses.

"See this that grown man shit right here. If you act right, you may be able to cuff a nigga," he teased. Flint squeezed her tightly then gave her a single kiss on her neck.

"Keep it up and I'ma cuff you alright," she tried her hand at some slick shit.

"Yeah, we'll see."

When he released her she drifted back a little and looked up at him like he was god. Flint flashed her those pearly whites and chuckled.

"I'll be right back," he said as he headed down the block.

Raven turned to her girls as she tried to contain the scream that was choking the hell out of her trying to break free. Jovanna and Breonni jumped in the back and Raven hopped in the front seat and started the car and turned on the air.

"Bitch, that muthafucka is smooth as hell," Breonni said as she unwrapped her lollipop.

"Oh, my god, did you hear that slick shit he was spiting. Girl, I'm scared," Raven said then burst out laughing.

"Don't get scared now. We about to show these niggas what happens when you fuck with a young bitch," Breonni said then slapped hands with Raven over the seat.

"Y'all crazy," Jovanna stated as she fumbled through her purse for her lip gloss.

"Oh, don't go there. Katina told us how your ass was all goo goo, ga ga over Shawn the other night when they snatched you up," Breonni revealed.

"That bitch talk too much," Jovanna laughed.

"Yeah, I thought so," Breonni said sitting back and looking over at the park.

"Turn on the music," Jovonna requested.

Raven started fumbling with the radio then they heard the screech of tires then four gunshots from up the block. The grey Cutlass sped past them and headed up the hill.

"What the fuck?" Breonni sat up looking at the scatter of niggas running across Elizabeth Avenue heading their way. A second car turned the corner blasting as niggas scattered and hit the ground behind parked cars.

Raven's eyes were quickly scanning the crowd in search of Flint. She saw him up the street with his gun fully extended popping off shots.

"Bitch, get down," Breonni yelled out.

Raven slid down slightly in her seat but kept her eyes still fixed on Flint. He aimed his gun at the fleeing vehicle and blasted out the back window sending glass flying everywhere. When she saw him double timing it in their direction she put her foot on the brake and then shifted the gear into drive.

"Y'all get the fuck outta here," he ordered then threw the gun in her lap and ran and jumped in an Expedition.

Raven didn't say a word she pulled out racing down to the light. She quickly tucked the gun under her leg and moved to 1&9. When she looked in the rearview mirror Jovanna was in the back seat in panic mode. Raven had to stay calm so she could think shit out. She drove all the way down until she got to the Raritan River, crossed the bridge, and went into an empty parking lot.

"What the fuck is you doing?" Jovanna asked, wanting her to keep on driving.

"I got this. Just chill," Raven half-shouted as she popped the trunk and got out.

"Bre, this bitch crazy," Jovanna said excitedly. She was looking around like the red and blues was hot on their ass.

"I ain't got shit to say," she said as she folded her arms and looked out the window.

Raven stared into the trunk planning her next move. She went back to the front seat, put the gun under her shirt, and then moved back to the trunk.

"I don't even know who this bitch is," Jovanna said with a nervous chuckle.

"You gonna learn today," Breonni said then looked back to see what was going on but with the trunk up she couldn't tell what Raven was doing back there.

Raven popped the clip out the Glock placed the gun and clip down in the trunk as she fumbled around looking for something to wipe it down with. She moved a sneaker box and found a small towel. She wiped everything off and then wrapped it in the towel.

She grabbed the towel in the cuff of her arm and slammed the trunk. "I'll be right back," she mouthed through the window then double timed it back to the side of the river and threw the gun in one direction and the bullets in the other. She rolled up the towel and tucked it under her arm. When she got back to the car Breonni was in the front seat and Jovanna was sitting up with her arms rested between the two seats starring at her.

"What?" asked Raven as if she didn't realize the severity of everything that had gone down.

"Bitch, who are you?" Breonni asked looking at her as if seeing her for the very first time. "What the fuck was you thinking? Got our asses all the way out here committing crimes and shit."

"I don't know. You know I be watching First 48. I just went into fugitive mode," she said then looked at them.

Jovanna looked at Breonni then back at Raven. After a few seconds of silence, they all burst out laughing.

"Girl, I need a drink and something to smoke. My nerves bad as hell," Breonni said, buckling her seat belt.

"Me, too."

Raven started the car and pulling back into traffic.

"Sit yo ass back. JoJo, we already riding dirty with Bonnie over here," Breonni said, shaking her head.

They shared a few more laughs as they rode back to the city. Raven dropped the girls off then drove to her house. When Raven pulled up to the curb the reality of the night began to take control of her body. Her hands started to shake as she pulled the key from the engine. Hot flashes emitted from her palms and sweat formed on her nose.

She jumped out of the car and ran inside.

"What the hell is wrong with you?" her father yelled out as he watched her fly pass.

"I have to pee," she yelled back, slamming the bathroom door.

Raven put her back against the door and slid to the floor. She looked down at her shaking hands and tried to take some deep breaths in order to calm down. She reached in her pocket and pulled out the key to Flint's BMW and stared at it long and hard wondering was the relationship that she had just begun with him going to be a blessing or a curse.

"Raven!" She could hear her father yelling form the other room like it was on fire.

"Yes, Daddy," she answered through the door.

"Come get this got-damn phone!"

"Shit," Raven said as she realized she left her phone in the car. Raven stood to her feet and snatched the door open and jogged down the hall. She took the cordless from her dad as she left the room trying to avoid his suspicious stare.

"Hello."

"You straight, ma?" Flint's voice boomed through the phone sending her body through a mix of emotion.

"Yes. I'm straight." Raven said as she walked in her room and closed the door.

"Sorry for putting you in that situation," he apologized.

"It's all good," Raven said lying across her bed.

"Can I come get you?"

"Yes."

"Good. I'm outside your house." Flint had just pulled

up and was scanning the area to make sure everything was copasetic.

Raven got quiet. Then she jumped up and looked out the window. Her eyes settled on the truck parked across the street. "Here I come." She disconnected the call, changed her shirt, brushed her teeth and headed outside.

"I'll be right back, Daddy," she said, darting pass him not giving him a chance to respond.

"You better be right back. You just walked your bonny ass in here," he yelled out as the door closed.

Raven walked over to the black truck that waited a few feet away. As she approached, Flint got out the passenger side and Hammer got out the driver's side.

"Give him my keys. Is the gun in the car?" Flint asked as he moved closer to her.

"No, I got rid of it," she whispered as she passed the tall, dark-skinned man the key.

Flint looked at her with one brow raised. "What you mean you got rid of it? What you do with it?"

"I threw it in the river out on 1&9. What? Was I supposed to ride around with a hot gun?" she answered matter-of-factly.

Flint stared at her for a few seconds.

"Come on," he said. He helped her into the truck and closed the door. He walked to the car, gave Hammer some instructions, retrieved her phone, and then jumped back into the truck and pulled off with Raven in the passenger seat. They drove in silence while Flint thought about what to say.

"I have to admit. I usually don't fuck with young girls and, to be honest, I was just out to see if I could be that nigga to hit first."

He looked over at her. Raven kept her gaze out the front window as she processed his words.

"But when a nigga out here in these streets he need a woman on his side that can ride with him. And you have more than proven that you deserve the opportunity to get at a nigga's heart. A man of my caliber would be a fool not to hold onto you," he continued as he whipped his truck through Lyons past the hospital.

Raven sat quietly listening to Flint. Her demeanor was calm but on the inside she wanted to do cartwheels. He could have tried to sell her socks with holes in them on the side of the road and she would have bought them. She carefully thought out her words. She wanted to make sure she didn't say anything stupid.

"I will say this. You're official and I definitely wanna rock with you. But you have to promise me that you will always protect me and keep me safe. And no matter what comes into our circle you gotta be honest with me."

She looked over at him as the car came to a stop.

"I can do that and I need the same from you," Flint responded.

Raven only nodded her head. She feared speaking would allow her emotions to take control. Flint leaned in took her by the back of her neck.

"Thank you," he said. Then, he kissed her deeply. When he pulled back her eyes were still closed and her heart was beating fast.

When she opened her eyes, he was smiling. Raven giggled then covered her face.

"Come on, I'm hungry as hell," he said breaking the

tension of their first intense moment.

"Me, too. Shit, this sidekick thing got my ribs touching my back," she joked.

"You crazy as hell," he said as they walked into Amin Halal Chinese Restaurant.

"You better know," she shot back.

Raven didn't know what lay ahead, but she did know she was going forward full speed. Whatever she encountered on this journey she was prepared to accept with open arms.

CHAPTER 13

A Promise is a Promise

The day had finally come. Raven, Jovonna, Bre, and Katina were running around getting ready for the prom. It had been a rough end of the school year. After starting to run with Long, Naseem, Flint, and Shawn, the girls' small worlds had become magnified. Breonni, Katina, and Jovonna had all just turned eighteen. Raven's birthday was only weeks away and tonight would be the kick off to their adult lives. Their relationships were moving fast. No longer shy little girls, all four were on the brink of becoming women. With the final details of their big night complete, they were ready to seal the deal.

"We will see y'all at eight," Raven said dropping Breonni and Katina off at the house.

"Bitch, you better be on time," Breonni threatened.

"Girl, get on the curb before you go to the prom with yo shit in a cast," she laughed as she watched Breonni shoot up her middle finger.

The two of them struggled up the stairs with their bags and damned near dropped everything on their way inside. When they got upstairs, their dresses and shoes were already laid out on Katina's queen size canopy bed and jewelry set up on the dresser. Quickly they undressed and hit separate showers. When Katina exited the master bathroom she took a seat in front of her vanity mirror wearing a sexy black two piece bra and thong set that Naseem had bought her and began taking the pins out of her curls. Breonni sat next to her on the bench and began to do the same.

"So are you ready for tonight?" Breonni asked smiling as she applied a thin coat of lipstick.

"I guess so," Katina said as she began to apply a lip gloss to her lips. "What about you?"

"Hell, yeah, but I'm scared though. That nigga is nothing to be played with."

Katina started to laugh, "Well, you asked for it."

"Whatever, bitch. I know your scary ass better not back out. We have a deal."

"I won't. I'ma give him whatever he wants," she responded thinking *if she only knew.*

Just as Breonni got ready to reveal something, Katina's mom came into the room holding her glass of white wine.

"Alright, ladies. The limo will be here in about forty-five minutes. I need to get y'all dressed and downstairs for pictures." she announced as she took a seat in a chair.

The girls stood up and began helping each other into their dresses.

Breonni wore a very thin pink, off one shoulder dress with a cream wrist clutch. Katina had on a cream dress in the same style accentuating her chocolate skin with a pink wrist clutch.

Once they were fully dressed, Katina's mom helped them with their jewelry.

"You look so beautiful. I am so blessed to be able to be here to get my baby ready," she said to Katina. She put her mother's diamond earrings onto Katina's ears and helped her with the matching necklace and bracelet. She thought back to the night that her mother put them onto her ears. Now that she was able to do the same for her daughter, tears welled up in her eyes.

Breonni watched mother and daughter interact. She felt happy for Katina but sad for herself. Her mom was too drunk to even care. Little did she know that Katina's mom had something special for her daughter's best friend.

"Come here, Bre. You know you are just like a daughter to me," she said. Katina's mom reached into a small bag and pulled out a box of earrings and a bracelet. "Now, I want you to take these moments and carry them with you. This is just the beginning you will go on to do great things."

She helped Breonni put on her new jewelry and hugged her tightly.

Katina was filled with pride. Somehow her mom always seemed to know the right thing to say and do, not just for her but for her friends as well.

"Thank you so much, Ma," Breonni said as she fought back the tears.

"Anytime. I am always here for you," she responded looking into Breonni's eyes and giving her a comforting smile. She wiped a tear from her eye and gave her one last hug.

"Now," she said flipping the script. "I know y'all got plans for tonight. I'm trusting you. The limo will be taking you to the prom then to Atlantic City. We got you a suite. Please enjoy yourselves and don't embarrass me."

"We're not, Ma," Katina said grabbing her overnight bag and placing a few last minute items into it.

"Yeah, okay. Don't get down there and fall on some dick."

"Maaaaa," Katina yelled out while Breonni burst out laughing.

"Sheeeit. I was eighteen once. Don't get it twisted," she said as she started picking up the empty bags and boxes.

"We will be on our best behavior," Breonni promised.

Katina's mom put some finishing touches on their hair and make-up. "Perfect," her mom said stepping back to look at them.

Katina picked up her bag headed towards the door. When they reached the stairs Katina's father was standing at the bottom with the video camera. They posed and smiled as he taped them before they took a series of photos.

"Aww, look at my princess," he said then kissed her cheek, "Love you."

"Love you, too, Daddy."

He kissed her forehead. "Here is a credit card. It has a five thousand dollar limit. Spend wisely, have fun."

The doorbell rang.

Katina's mom turned to answer the door. She looked out the peephole to see the chauffer standing in his black suit and hat. Lynette pulled the door open.

"Good evening," she greeted him with a smile.

"I'm here for the Miss Katina," he announced then escorted the girls to the white Mercedes stretch limo.

"Look at this," Breonni said rubbing on the leather

seats.

"This is nice," Katina announced taking in the interior.

When the girls were comfortably inside the limo, Katina's dad snapped a few more pictures.

"Have a fun," he encouraged.

Then, they were off. The limo stopped to pick up Raven, then Jovonna.

Jovanna and Raven had on tuxedo style knee length dresses that came up to the neck with their shoulders out. Jovonna's dress was pink with cream up the front and Raven's was cream with pink up the front. The crowd in front of Jovonna's house made it almost impossible to get down the street. She jumped into the limo with her family snapping pictures and yelling out well wishes as the driver closed the door.

"We royalty tonight," Jovonna sang out dancing in her seat.

Breonni reached over and grabbed a bottle of Sparkling Apple Cider by the neck.

"No we bossy tonight," Katina said as she pretended to drink from the bottle.

Katina threw her head back and laughed. Raven grabbed a glass and crossed her legs. "Hook a bitch up," she said with her pinky out.

Breonni turned on the satellite radio to the hip hop station and began to jam. She opened the cider, poured them each a glass, and they toasted to the night. The party was officially on. The girls talked and giggled all the way to the venue. When they pulled up, they took a minute to remind themselves of the promise they took.

"No turning back now," Breonni said.

"Tonight all bets are off," Raven announced.

"And, so are these panties," Breonni joked and they all erupted in laughter.

Katina just smiled knowing she had already violated the code but she wasn't planning to tell her girls until after they had all gone through with it.

"Love y'all so much," Jovonna said.

"Aww, JoJo. We love you, too," they sang in unison. Then, they had a group hug.

"Alright. Enough of this mushy shit. Let's go stunt on these bitches."

Breonni reached for the door and they stepped out one by one. All eyes were on the four girls. They strutted down the red carpet style entrance with people snapping pictures the whole time.

When they got inside, the dining hall was nicely decorated in black, white and grey. The crisp white tablecloths held beautiful china and silverware with vases of red roses in the center. A huge monitor flashed pictures of the year's happy moments. The girls' faces lit up when they saw several flicks of them acting up and having fun. The DJ was on point and they couldn't wait to get it poppin'.

The girls claimed a table up front then ran to the bathroom to freshen up before they hit the dance floor. They partied hard all night only stopping to take pictures and share a few laughs. Of course, niggas were pushing up on them but they turned them all down. They already had some beasts waiting on them. The girls couldn't wait to get to them.

When the party was over, they said their last goodbyes then headed outside. As prearranged, Flint, Naseem,

Long, and Shawn were right there waiting for them. The girls walked over to the vehicles full of pride. Naseem smiled broadly when he saw Katina.

"Hey, baby. You look beautiful." He said as he leaned in to kiss her.

"Thank you, baby," she responded.

"Get your things from the limo so we can bounce," Naseem instructed releasing her from his grip.

While the girls gathered their things and headed back to the cars, Naseem hit the limo driver off with a few stacks. The driver smiled, hopped back into the limo, and pulled away.

Long took Breonni by the hand as he placed her bags in the trunk. "You know you in trouble tonight, right?"

"You're the one in trouble," she slickly stated as she took her seat in the car.

Flint and Shawn followed suit putting Raven and Jovonna in their cars. All eyes were on them as they left. Females pointed and whispered. Breonni, in true diva form, was in heaven. She threw up her hand and gave those jealous bitches the princess wave.

CHAPTER 14

Place Your Bet

The four cars pulled up to the valet of the Tropicana Hotel one behind the other. Naseem jumped out first, handed the middle-aged, uniformed man his keys and a fifty dollar bill, and then he opened the door for Katina. When she stepped out of the vehicle her eyes darted from here to there drinking in everything. *Atlantic City is so beautiful at night* she thought looking up at the top of the Tropicana sign. The bright lights put her into party mode.

Breonni and Raven couldn't contain themselves any longer they sprang out of the passenger seats of Long and Flint's whips and rushed over to each other. They began to joke and point at a few scantily dressed women wearing very high heels and bad wigs who were entering the hotel lobby.

"You know them bitches here to fuck," Breonni judged.

"So are we," Raven reminded her a little over a whisper.

Breonni looked at her. "Bitch, don't judge me," she said flippantly.

"I'm just saying," Raven shrugged.

The two resumed talking shit about the array of people milling about and going in and out of the hotel.

"Bitch, you crazy," Raven laughed as they walked toward Katina.

Flint and Long grabbed the bags from the trunk before handing over their keys to valet and heading to the curb. Jovonna, who was with Shawn, finally exited his vehicle. The nervousness in her eyes made Katina uncomfortable. The smile dropped from Katina's face and her gut filled with concern for her girl. Jovonna could mask her fears with Bre and Raven but with Katina it was almost impossible.

"Let me go help, JoJo," Katina interrupted the banter and walked off.

When she reached Jovonna, she rested her hand on her shoulder and quietly asked. "Are you okay?"

Jovonna forced a smile. "Yeah, I'm good," she lied.

"Don't be scared, girl. We will all be in the same boat," Katina tried to comfort her.

"Yeah, I know, with some big ass paddles," Jovanna joked holding her hands about a foot apart.

Katina's eyes got big and her hand shot up to her mouth. Jovonna laughed and hugged Katina. The moment they'd just shared put her mind more at ease.

"Thank you," she said sincerely.

"You're welcome. Come on." Katina flashed a reassuring smile then grabbed her arm and led her to where everyone else stood. When the couples walked into the hotel lobby, Katina checked her and Naseem into the suite that her mom had booked while Long, Shawn and Flint secured the other three rooms.

"It's about to go down," Breonni said and did a little dance in place.

"You need help," Jovonna blushed shaking her head.

"Not now, but later tonight. I may need a full body cast," she joked.

"You stupid," Raven said as the rest of the crew came up behind them.

Moving to the elevator each of the girls experienced an onslaught of emotions: joy about their accomplishments but fear and uncertainty about what was going to happen from tonight on.

The elevator began its assent then stopping on the third floor where Breonni and Long got off and headed to their room.

"See y'all downstairs." Breonni lifted her eyebrows up and down.

"Girl, bye," Raven said as the elevator doors began to close.

Raven and Flint and Shawn and Jovanna had adjoining rooms on the fifth floor. The elevator doors opened and they stepped off.

"Don't get caught up. Be downstairs in thirty minutes. I'm hungry as hell," Naseem instructed.

"Nigga, you got something to snack on fall back," Long teased knowing the secret that was hidden from everyone else.

"Fuck you, nigga," Naseem yelled out as the doors slid closed.

Katina looked up at Naseem as the elevator moved upwards. He shrugged his shoulders and remained quiet.

When they reached the top floor he took her by the

hand and led her off the elevator. "It's all good, little mama," he said.

"Um, hmm, I bet it is," she replied as they headed down the carpeted hall.

The moment Naseem and Katina stepped into their suite Katina's eyes danced around the room. The relaxing tones of tan and brown perfected the decor. She set her bag down and moved to the window and looked out at the ocean. Naseem walked off to the bedroom with their bags giving her a few minutes to enjoy the view.

Naseem laid his clothes out on the bed then joined Katina at the window. He wrapped his arms around her and nuzzled his nose in the crook of her neck inhaling the seductive fragrance of her perfume.

Katina leaned back against his chest and enjoyed the feel of his body pressed against hers. "You know tonight was supposed to be my first night," Katina said softly and with a hint of regret.

Naseem saw her regret. "My bad. I would have waited but you kept asking for it," he half-joked. Then, he bent down and kissed her neck.

"Yeah, right. You took it."

"I damn sure did and I'ma take a whole lot more tonight," he stated with confidence. "Come shower with me so we can get ready to go to dinner."

Naseem squeezed her booty.

Katina giggled as he took her hand and led her to the bathroom.

TAINTED

* * * * *

"Come on, Ma. They waiting for us," Flint said as he poured himself a drink.

"Here I come," Raven called out from the bathroom as she pulled her dress over her head. She nervously fidgeted with her clothes and took a hard look at herself in the mirror. She and Flint had almost gone there but some unforeseen circumstances had prevented it. Tonight she would have to be a big girl and give him what he wanted. Raven took a few deep breaths and then walked out the bathroom.

"Look at you all sexy in that sundress." Flint gave her a smile.

Raven twirled around in her white strapless dress and smiled when her eyes met his. "Come mere," he said pulling the stool from the bar and taking a seat.

Raven walked over to where he sat and stood between his legs.

Flint put his hand around her back. "I know tonight is very special for you and I am going to do my best to give you some very happy memories." He thought about the few times he'd tried to convince her to be with him and the awkward moments it had caused.

"Thank you, baby."

Raven wrapped her arms around his neck and kissed his lips. The heat coming off her body caused his dick to jump.

"Don't wake up my friend. You gonna miss your little dinner party."

He pulled her into him.

"Oh, boy, come on." She moved his hands and backed away before they went too far.

Raven moved to the nightstand to grab her purse and watched Flint grab his gun, tuck it in his waist, and then place his money in his pocket.

When they got downstairs all the other couples were seated with drinks in front of them.

"What took y'all so long?" Breonni gave them the side eye.

"You know how your girl do," Flint reminded.

"Yes, I do." She looked up at Raven. "Sit next to me. We ordered already. This is yours." Breonni moved the virgin Pina Colada in front of Raven's spot.

"Thanks, mama," she said taking a seat next to Breonni. She took a sip of her drink then grabbed her menu.

"This place is pretty nice." Raven's eyes darted around the dining hall.

"It's alright. They better have good dessert." Breonni grabbed the small dessert menu from the center of the table.

Long slid his hand onto her lap and whispered in her ear causing her to blush and giggle nervously. Breonni didn't dare respond. She squeezed her legs closed as he moved back. She was ready to put whatever he requested in his mouth as soon as she could.

When the waitress returned, Raven placed her order and the girls began reminiscing about special moments earlier in night. In between casual statements, Katina noticed Naseem checking his phone then leaning over and whispering in Long's ear. It appeared that their little get away was both business and pleasure.

The meals arrived and the aroma of steak smothered with mushrooms and sautéed shrimp, baked potatoes and butter deliciously filled the area as each plate was positioned in its place. Wasting no time, everyone picked up their utensils and began to dig in.

When it was time for dessert Breonni ordered herself a big piece of Chocolate Mousse cake. When the waitress returned she had several staff members with her each carrying a slice for each girl with a candle in it as Naseem had previously arranged. They surrounded the table clapping and smiling in celebration of their big night.

The girls' faces lit up with excitement. When the waitresses left the table they looked at each other with gleam in their eyes.

"Ready?" Katina asked.

"Yes, let's go," Raven answered for all of them.

"One, two, three," Katina said looking around at her girls.

The girls closed their eyes, made their wishes, and blew out their candles.

"Thank you, babe," Katina said turning to Naseem and kissing his lips.

"Anything for you," he responded looking into her eyes.

"Cut that shit out," Breonni said and threw her napkin at them.

"Stop hating," Katina threw it back.

Breonni knocked it down before it hit her. "That's why you missed," she teased.

Peace and celebratory energy took over as the girls laughed and enjoyed their cake. Flint pulled Raven close to him as she chomped away. Shawn watched the interaction of each couple and could see that there was a genuine affection and respect. In his case, he really was just along for the ride.

After the tab was paid they all headed down the Boardwalk to enjoy some of the night life. The first spot they hit was the amusement parks.

"I wanna hit them rides," Jovonna said pulling Shawn by the arm.

"I want to race. Fuck that. I need to spank that ass," Raven said to Flint rubbing her hands together.

"Yo, ass can't drive," Flint shot back.

"Let's bet on it. A hundred dollars."

She threw up her pinky to seal the deal.

"I'ma spank that ass."

Flint grabbed her little pinky then headed to the entrance.

Naseem and Katina joined them at race cars and Shawn and Jovonna headed to the rides.

When the first race was over, Raven jumped out of her car and started talking shit. "What? Don't come for me," she excitedly ranted.

"Little mama, can handle a whip," Naseem said to Flint as he tried to recover from Raven putting dust in his face.

"Her ass think she *Fast and Furious*," Flint responded as he watched Raven celebrate.

"She cheated. She was all over the place." Katina cocked her head to the side pretending to be sad about the loss.

"Aww, look at my baby." Naseem played into her mood.

"Let's go meet up with Shawn and JoJo. And run me

my money playa," Raven gloated.

Flint went in his pocket and passed her a few bills. Raven held it up to the light. "Yeah we good," she joked as they headed to the meet the others.

The couples enjoyed a few more rides and games then headed to the beach. They held hands and talked and looked out over the water.

Naseem and Katina hugged and made promises to each that they would try their best to keep. Flint and Raven were also in a world of their own hugged up smiling and whispering. Breonni and Long did their regular; joked and acted like best friends.

However, Jovonna seemed slightly unhappy. Even though she laughed and talked with Shawn gaily, between the happy moments were seconds of complete silence that hid a pain she refused to share.

CHAPTER 15

Everything Is Not What It Seems

As the couples headed back to their rooms Katina tried to read her girls. Even though there were smiles on their faces she knew that slight fear filled their bellies. For Naseem and her the evening would be filled with all the things they loved about pleasing each other but she knew that her friends were going to be dealing with some of the emotions that came with a girl's first time.

As soon as Naseem and Katina entered their room, he set the mood. He pulled off his clothes, placed his phone on the docking station and hit his playlist.

"Let me freshen up real quick," Katina said as she seductively pulled her shirt over her head on her way to the bathroom.

Leaving the door open, Katina undressed and stepped in the shower. Carefully lathering her skin she filled her mind with thoughts of how good every touch of Naseem's hands would feel as they explored her body.

Naseem could see her silhouette through the shower curtain. The curve of her body seemed to be calling him.

Before he knew it, his feet were moving in her direction. His thuggish heart was beating fast in his chest. When he stepped into the shower, his man was full grown. Naseem slowly stroking his dick in his hand. Katina turned to see that steel and that hunger in his eyes. She placed her hands on his chest and softly kissed his firm pecks.

"I need that pussy on my tongue," said Naseem on heavy breath.

"You can have it wherever you want it, baby."

She looked up into his commanding brown eyes and got lost in their desire. It felt real good to be wanted so badly.

Naseem picked her up and placed her against the wall with her legs draped gracefully over his shoulders. Katina held on tight as he began to make love to her clit with the tip of his tongue. Naseem took her from one level of pleasure to another while she called out to be free from his grip. Katina could hardly breathe.

"I love you," was all she could say as he began to bring on the rain.

She closed her eyes and let it go.

"Oh, my god," she cried out gripping the back of his head with both hands.

Naseem rubbed his lips in her warm juices as her body jerked with every motion. With his first task complete he let her down and prepared his mind for what he had planned next. They rinsed their bodies and stepped out wrapping themselves in a towel.

Naseem walked Katina to the foot of the bed and carefully removed her towel allowing it to fall to the floor. He sucked her nipples gently while rubbing his hand between her thighs.

"No, baby, tonight I want to please you," she panted.

Naseem licked his lips and gave her a sneaky grin. He got into the middle of the bed and put his hands behind his head. He looked on as Katina kissed and licked her way to his thickness. She ran her tongue up his shaft then sucked gently on the head of his dick. Katina's wet, warm jaw action had Naseem's stomach filled with excitement as he watched his baby give him head for the first time. Even with her inexperience she had a nigga's toes twitching.

Katina licked and sucked until she heard a slight hiss leave his lips then she climbed up on him pressing her wet kitty against his pulsating pole, she grabbed it in her hand and slid down on it slow.

"Ahhh…" she moaned as his length filled her up.

Totally naked, Katina rode him to the beat of her heart as Brian McKnight *I Never Felt this Way* played softly in the background.

There will never come a day.
you'll ever hear me say that I want and need
to be without you.
I want to give my all. Baby, just hold me.
Simply control me.
'Cuz your arms, they keep away the lonelies.
When I look into your eyes
then I realize that all I need is you in my life.
All I need is you in my life.
Cuz I've never felt this way about lovin'.

Katina gripped the headboard as she moved gracefully up and down wetting him with every movement. Naseem held her in place and stroked up matching her rhythm.

Her moans almost drowned out the music as she dropped her head and squeezed her pussy muscles grabbing him tighter with every push. Nothing else existed but their budding love and Naseem giving it to her hard and deep.

* * * * *

In Room 315, the pleasurable art of the sixty-nine was well underway. Long and Breonni had become the oral sex freaks of the crew. Their chocolate bodies intertwined setting each other ablaze.

However, room 500, labored under a cloud of depression. Jovonna looked over at a disappointed Shawn who had given up after the second try. Jovonna was much different than her girls. She was very frigid and gave him every form of resistance she could muster. When Shawn realized that she wasn't planning on giving it up, he got out of bed, threw on his boxers, grabbed the bottle of Jack, and went to the couch.

Jovonna pulled the covers up to her neck and cried. She wanted to give herself to him but his nonchalant attitude made her nervous and hesitant. Her nerves caused more pain every time he touched her. She started to go after him and let him try again but she knew the liquor in his system would only cause him to tear into her without care or caution. Resigned to a terrible night she turned over and soon cried herself to sleep.

* * * * *

Room 501 would have a unique story to tell. Flint and Raven had taken each other there before their clothes even touched the floor. When their hot bodies hit the sheets Raven's body damn near begged Flint to do whatever he wanted.

Flint positioned his face between her legs and began to give her what she craved. Raven gripped the back of his head and arched her back as he licked and sucked to her pleasure. As she felt the pleasurable sensations taking control of her mind she looked down to see her baby but a distorted vision of her father replaced Flint's sexy face. Raven closed her eyes tightly as the orgasm took over her body. Flint's moans filled her ears as he enjoyed the taste of her sweetness.

Again, Raven opened her eyes. This time the vision was stronger as she released in Flint's mouth. The haunting memories of her past flooded her thoughts.

"Stop," she whispered as she pushed back from his grip.

"Nah, ma, I need you to come again," Flint whispered placing his mouth over her clit sucking gently as his tongue circled her pearl.

"No, please stop!" She pushed at his head but he continued to try to take her higher.

Raven squeezed her eyes tighter as she tried to erase the voice and images of her father's tainted love she had been enduring for years. Flint's whispered passion became her father's conniving voice; his gentle hands turned into Daddy's unwanted touch. Tears trickled from her eyes and her stomach bubbled with vomit that threatened to rush up. She looked down at Flint and tried to push Daddy out of her mind. She was torn between the feelings of pleasure and shame. Her mind screamed out *no* while her body screamed out *yes*. With one stroke of his tongue he was a boyfriend, and the next stroke he became Glen...not her lover but Daddy. On the brink of heaven and hell she squirmed to get free from Flint's hold.

Flint misread her body. He had no way of knowing what was going on inside her head. When he spread her legs wider and sucked harder on her clit Raven screamed and shoved him away from her.

"Stop, Daddy!" she cried.

Flint's head shot up as Raven backed up to the headboard shaking and crying. She gripped the pillow between her legs and squeezed it tight. Raven looked down at him covering her mouth as the tears rushed from her eyes and the pain pushed from her soul.

"Baby, you alright?" Flint asked. He was completely confused.

Raven shook her head from side to side. "No, I am not alright and I don't think I will ever be alright," she whispered.

Flint didn't understand what was wrong but he knew that whatever had a hold on her was beyond his repair. He moved to where she lay, pulled the covers over them, and cradled her in his arms.

"It's alright, ma. Let it out. I got you," he tried to comfort her.

"I'm sorry," she whined as she rested her head on his chest. Tears cascaded down her face onto his bare skin.

"No, baby, I'm sorry that what ever happened to you has you in so much pain."

"I will get better. I promise," she vowed as she put her arm around him.

Flint wiped her tears. "You don't have to be strong

for me. I got you. Tonight let me be *your* strength," he consoled then pulled her snug against his chest.

Flint's thoughts were all over the place. He wanted to make all her pain disappear but he didn't know how and she wasn't saying who or what had caused it. Had she just been a bitch off the block she would have had to fuck or fight. Tears had never been Flint's weakness but, for some reason, Raven's pain touched his gansta heart. He wanted to avenge whatever had happen to her.

"I'm not going to pressure you to tell me what happened. Just give me a name and I'll fix it," he offered.

"Today I can't. But when I do, you have to promise not to let it change the way you treat me." Raven sniffled as they stared into each other's eyes.

Flint nodded his agreement because he knew that there was nothing he could say to help heal her wound.

* * * * *

Breonni stared at Long as he walked out the bathroom in a towel, applied lotion to his skin then got dressed.

"Where you going?" she asked from her reclined position on the bed.

"You know what happens when duty calls." He walked over to the bed and kissed her lips. "I'll see you in the morning. Be good."

"What can I possibly get into?" she asked giving him a look of disappointment.

Long lifted one of his brows with a suspicious gleam in his eye. "I don't know. But whatever it is scratch that shit from your list."

"Whatever. Just leave the money on the night stand, Big Daddy," she joked.

"You crazy as hell," he chuckled.

"I know but you love me," she said putting her hand out.

Long chuckled as he dropped a couple hundred dollars in her lap. "Stay up here, ma. I don't want you roaming around. Plus, I need to taste you again when I walk through the door." He kissed her once more before grabbing his tool and heading out. Breonni shook her head, put the pillow over her face, and screamed. When she removed it she threw it across the room. Her plans of becoming a woman had failed again. Earlier, Long had eaten her pussy in twenty different ways but he gave her no dick. The very thing she was craving he was holding back. *But why?* she thought as she got out of the bed and headed to the shower.

* * * * *

Naseem watched Katina sleep. He eased around the room collecting his things being careful not to wake her. As he exited the room to meet up with Long, he ran the game plan through his mind. Tonight they were having a sit down with the Boss. They were going to lay all their cards on the table. It was time to take their organization to a whole new level.

Long saw Naseem emerging from the elevator and headed in his direction. They were taking a chance calling for a meeting but they wanted to get to the top. Staying in the background was not going to give him the boss status he craved. Naseem needed to make moves, too. He wanted to be his own man. Standing in his brother's shadow was not acceptable.

The two men moved swiftly through the Casino looking for the table the Boss was supposed to occupy. After going from one side of the casino to the other Naseem grabbed his phone and placed the call.

"Hello," the female voice rang through the phone.

"Is Kayson available?" Naseem asked.

"Turn around and head to the table in the corner that is roped off," the voice instructed right before the line went dead.

Naseem took the phone away from his ear and turned around. Long looked in the direction of his gaze. Across the room sat one of the most beautiful chocolate women he had ever seen. His eyes were pleased but his mind was confused. The meeting called for a sit down with *men* so why had they sent in a bitch?

"What the fuck is up with this shit?" Naseem uttered the words that Long was thinking.

"I was thinking the same thing. What the fuck they try-ing to play us out?" Long asked as he stood contemplating whether to go over to the table or bounce.

KoKo raised her glass and nodded her head signaling them to come to her. Naseem accepted her request and headed in her direction. Naseem and Long cautiously stepped to the guarded area. Naseem gripped the bag of money tightly in his hand as he was patted down by two men in KoKo's small entourage.

"Have a seat," a tall bald man instructed looking at Naseem with a creased brow and steady eye.

Naseem took a seat at the table while Long was given the same treatment. Long rested his arms at his side then pulled out a chair and took a seat next to Naseem.

After a few seconds of silence Naseem looked over at Long, and then turned in the direction of the woman.

"So, what can I do for you?" KoKo asked sitting back in her seat with her legs crossed.

Long looked over her curves in her all white pants suit that perfectly fit her chocolate frame. He was taken in by her beauty.

"Baseem said he had some work he needed us to do. I wanted to let him know that we are ready," Naseem replied as he tried to adjust to the idea that he was sitting there talking to a woman about business.

KoKo nodded her head. "So, what is it that you are ready for?" She wore a smug grin on her face.

Naseem began to get an uneasy feeling in his stomach. He stroked his chin for a minute then decided that he needed to end the meeting because he was not planning on negotiating with no bitch. "I thank you for taking the time to meet with me but it was my understanding that I was meeting with the Boss."

"I am the Boss," KoKo said taking her glass into her hand.

"No disrespect but I was planning on talking to Kayson," Naseem shot back.

"Who the fuck is this nigga that Baseem done sat in front of me?" KoKo looked over and asked Chucky with a sinister chuckle.

He gave her a half smile and put his hands up as if to say *It's your show*. KoKo nodded as she looked at Naseem.

The crease in her forehead deepened. His ass was definitely about to get it.

"Let me explain something to you. Baseem don't run shit. Every decision that is made comes across my desk. Don't ever throw your dick on the table when you're dealing with me. It ain't long enough."

KoKo leaned forward and folded her hands in front of her, as she locked eyes with Naseem.

"Now, I respect your get down but this organization has two bosses and I am the other one and no doubt the baddest bitch you will ever lay eyes on."

Naseem held firm eye contact while talking himself down. He knew what he was capable of and submitting to pussy was not part of his get down.

"Tell Kayson when he's ready I'm ready," he said as he started to rise from his seat.

"I wouldn't pass your message if it had weed in the middle and fire on the end. Fuck outta here," KoKo spat putting her security on point. The meeting had gone way past uncomfortable.

Long looked at the sexy, evil yet calm way she handled herself and was impressed. He could see that she was the type of bitch a man could bow to yet make *her* bow when necessary. He reached over and put his hand on Naseem's forearm.

Naseem turned in his direction as he battled with the idea of cussing her out and taking his chances at getting past the goons that stood behind him ready to flex.

"If I may," Long cut in trying to take control of the situation.

KoKo looked over at him giving him an opportunity

to speak.

"First, let me say thank you for taking time to meet with us. Secondly, we are at your disposal for whatever you may need." He reached down and grabbed the bag of money and brought it to his lap. "Here is our weekly quota plus interest. We wanted to get it out the way."

Long caught her gaze and her attention as he moved to pass her the bag. KoKo raised her hand up to stop his movement.

"You can put it back on the floor and please continue."

Long placed the bag on the floor and sat back in his seat. "I know your time is valuable so I'm not going to hold you. However, if you need anything at any time just holla," he said then rose to his feet.

Naseem began to stand as well. He was steaming but was careful not to throw gas on an already smoldering flame.

KoKo was impressed with Long's effort to try and calm her down, but he underestimated the fact that she was not the type of woman you could win with foreplay. She liked it raw and rough. All he did was expose that his boy had weakness and KoKo was going to use Long's strength to her advantage.

"Before you go…," she started.

The urgency in her voice stopped them in their tracks.

"…I do have something for you to do. But you will have to come alone. Your boy's attitude speaks to my trigger finger and this bitch is diabolical." KoKo rubbed her hands together looking up at them both.

Naseem's body language confirmed his anger and inability to work with her.

"I'll send for you soon, Long. In the meantime get your boy right. You're dismissed," she said sitting back in her seat.

"I'll be ready," Long accepted her invitation.

"Oh, yeah, find out who your enemies are because if left living they will rise up to destroy you," she warned.

Naseem remained quiet. He was ready to blow and didn't trust his tongue to deliver the proper response.

"Have a safe trip," Long extended his final words and then headed out of her area.

"You do the same," KoKo said as they walked away.

When they were out of earshot Naseem looked at Long as they headed to the elevator. "What the fuck just happened? That bitch is crazy."

"It's all good. That right there is pussy with power. You gotta stroke it before you run up in it," he said as his wheels started to turn.

Naseem didn't give a fuck who she was. He wasn't fucking with her on any level.

"I'ma need to holla at Baseem. I *can't* with that bitch," he emphasized as they walked on the elevator.

"Nigga, it's all good. Let's go blow some money," replied Long.

KoKo picked up her phone as she processed the interaction she had with Naseem and Long.

"Hello," Baseem answered.

"Yeah, I met your brother."

"How was it?" Baseem sat up at his desk.

"I can't fuck with him. He's too sensitive. But that

nigga, Long, I can use him. Bring him to me in a couple weeks. I have the perfect thing for him to do."

"I got you," he said then disconnected the call.

KoKo grabbed her drink and sat back. Her mind went to the evil plan she was setting into motion. Long had just volunteered himself for a suicide mission and she was going to accept his offer.

CHAPTER 16

The Morning After

It was Monday, late afternoon following prom weekend, and Katina was walking up Day Street headed to Breonni's building. As she approached, she saw Jovonna and Raven sitting on the stoop.

"Why y'all sitting out here?" Katina asked.

"You know that bitch ain't up yet," Raven said popping her gum.

"Come on. I am not standing out here," Katina said as she noticed a couple of dudes staring them down and coming their way. They jumped up and hurried inside the building.

Buzz. Buzz. Buzz. Katina was leaning on the buzzer.

"Hold on, yo," a male's voice came through the door then the locks clicked. The door swung open. "What's up?" asked Mike Breonni's perverted older brother.

As usual, he ogled them with lust-filled eyes. He had on the same musty looking grey sweat pants from Friday that hung off his boney frame.

"Move boy," Raven scoffed pushing him to the side.

"You know you love me." Mike smacked her butt as she walked by.

"Stop! Get on my nerves!" she yelled, smacked his arm, and then ran to Breonni's room.

Jovonna and Katina used the distraction to hurry pass. Breonni's brother was the definition of a thirsty nigga. Jovonna looked down at Breonni's mom passed out drunk on the couch and turned up her nose. She was also in the same clothes and in the same spot they left her in on Friday.

Raven turned on the light and plopped on the bed. "What the fuck?" Breonni asked as she took her head from under the covers.

"Get up, bitch. The day is almost over." Raven snatched the cover off of her.

"Y'all bitches get on my nerves," Breonni said sitting up and stretching.

She looked over at Katina and Jovonna who had taken a seat on the day bed across from her. She pointed at Raven. "Why y'all bring crazy to my house?" she asked rising to her feet.

"Oh, Lord, put some clothes on." Raven frowned. Breonni had on nothing but a thong.

"That's what your ass get. I bet you'll think twice before you pull a bitch covers off," Breonni chastised.

Jovonna and Katina just laughed.

"JoJo," Breonni sang as she grabbed a t-shirt out of her drawer.

"Hey, Bre," Jovonna shot back with a shy look.

"Tina, Tina, Tina," she sang now starting with Katina.

"Hey, Breonni," Katina said with a sly smirk on her face.

"Bitch, you know I am not talking to you." she joked.

"Why? What I do?" Katina asked with a puzzled look on her face.

"You broke the code. We had a pact and you broke it."

Jovonna and Raven's heads snapped around to look at her. "What you talking about Bre?" Raven asked.

"Tell 'em Tina," she said, hopping up on her dresser.

"Yeah, tell us Tina," Jovonna said as she stood up placing her hands on her hips.

Katina put her face in her hands took a deep breath then smiled. "I have been having sex with Nas for the past month," she confessed.

"What?" Jovonna exclaimed with an attitude.

"I'm not mad at you, girl. That nigga is fine as hell." Raven said.

"Nah, fuck that. We had a promise," Jovonna stood up and paced back and forth.

"Girl, bye. I would have broke, too. With all that fine in my face," Raven said as she hopped up on the dresser next to Breonni.

"You broke, too. Didn't you?" Breonni asked Raven.

Raven smiled. "Girl, I couldn't help it," she lied then burst out laughing.

"Y'all bitches ain't right. Here I am all fucked up ready to go soak in the tub and y'all been fucking for weeks," Jovanna said, giving them the dirty look. She fought hard to mask her lie because just like Raven she had not yet broken the promise.

"Sorry, JoJo." Katina leaned over and attempted to hug her.

"Oh no. Don't hug me now," she said as she playfully

pushed away.

"Well, all y'all owe me money because I still didn't give it up. I want my shit tomorrow," Breonni cut in.

"Oh, bitch, please. You gave it up," Raven disputed. She hopped off the dresser to go look into the shopping bags that she saw piled in the corner.

"For your information, I did not. We went shopping, ate, and chilled at the hotel."

"Hold up. You mean to tell me you ain't give him nothing?" Jovanna asked lips twisted and head to the side.

"Nope. I am still the only good girl in the crew."

Breonni folded her arms across her chest.

"Like I said, bitch, please. You been sucking that nigga's dick like it's the cure for cancer," Raven said not looking up from the bags.

Katina gasped and covered her mouth, "Ohhhh. You have?"

"Girl, bye. We all been doing that shit since junior high." Breonni said and waved her hand.

"No, bitch, *you* been doing that shit," Jovanna burst out laughing, pointed at the bags, and continued, "And shit if he passing off like this and that's all you doing, then we need to pay her ass for some lessons."

They all erupted in laughter and nodded their heads in agreement.

"Whatever. Let's get these details flowing through the room. Shit, I gotta feel like I got some, too." Breonni jumped down and dove onto her bed.

"JoJo grab that ashtray from under the bed and let's get this shit poppin'."

She folded her legs up under her in anticipation of

hearing the juicy details.

For the next two hours, the girls laughed and compared stories. The bond between the friends was still solid as a rock. With the new territory they were now covering they were stepping into womanhood together.

"We can't ever let anything come between us," Breonni said in all seriousness. "No matter who we are with or where we go we have to always be there for each other. And we can't ever let a nigga dictate our friendship."

"Never," Jovonna confirmed.

"Only death," Raven chimed in.

As usual, Katina got choked up and walked over to them and grabbed every one for a group hug.

"No matter what. Our bond will never be broken," she vowed hugging them tightly.

CHAPTER 17

Broken

As Baseem drove to Hoboken to meet Naseem, the past ran through his mind. No doubt his brother was solid but his actions suggested that maybe Baseem had made a mistake trying to bring him into the big leagues. He had already warned Naseem that the shit he was involved in was for men of iron. Naseem had displayed to KoKo that he was bendable. Baseem was putting his reputation on the line to bring his younger brother into the family. He had worked too hard to prove his loyalty. He damned sure was not going to allow Naseem to fuck that up.

When he pulled up next to Naseem's truck he turned his music off and stepped out of his vehicle quickly. Naseem jumped out of the truck and tried to adjust his attitude. The urgency of Baseem's call let him know that KoKo had put something hot in his ear. He knew Baseem was getting ready to express it straight, no chaser.

"What the fuck is wrong with you?" Baseem asked as he approached Naseem.

"You tell me. You seem like you already made your

mind up about the situation," Naseem responded.

"Don't fucking play with me. I told you that this right here is big boy status. You still thinking like a block hustla. This right here will split your shit wide open," Baseem spat looking at the nonchalant expression on his brother's face.

"You know I don't like fucking with bitches in business," Naseem said. He was beginning to heat up.

Baseem got into Naseem's face. "Let me share some shit with you right quick. There may be pussy between those thighs but that bitch right there is tried and proven. When you were running small plastic for the next niggas she was putting muthafuckas on they ass."

Baseem's voice took on a venomous tone. "That woman *is* the organization… fuck is wrong with you?"

Naseem stood breathing heavily as he looked at the anger burning in his brother's eyes like hot coals. He thought for a few seconds then carefully chose his words before speaking.

"A'ight I feel you. I'ma straighten it up," he conceded to his brother's point.

"Ain't no making it right. You gotta go through Long now. She don't want to see your fucking face. For now, just fall back."

Baseem turned to leave.

"Hold the fuck up. What you mean go through Long? This is my shit," Naseem tried to boss up.

Baseem turned back to his brother. "You still think this shit is a game," he said with a slight chuckle. "Let me make this shit plain. In this family, loyalty is earned. It's never just given."

Baseem watched the color change in his brother's face.

"The next time you come into the presence of a real boss keep your mouth shut and your ears open. You might learn something."

This time, when Baseem turned away, he didn't look back.

"I'll be in touch," he said with finality.

Baseem slid behind the wheel of his whip, slammed the door, and peeled out the parking lot sending rocks and gravel flying out from under his screeching tires.

Naseem ran his hand over his face and leaned against his vehicle. He knew that it was going to be hard for his brother and him to forgive everything between them and move forward but he never thought he would see the day that another bitch would come between them.

Naseem hopped into his car and headed to see Long. At this point, he didn't give a fuck who was in charge. If he had to fall back, he would but he would still be the one pulling the strings.

* * * * *

Flint and Raven were becoming closer by the day. She knew that if she wanted to keep seeing him she had to introduce him to her father. She called him up and asked him to be sure to come inside when he picked her up tonight.

As she moved nervously around the house getting ready Glen eyed her with a scowl on his face. "You going out with that nigga again?" Her dad yelled out from his worn out lounge chair in the family room.

"Yes, Daddy," she said as she placed his plate on the TV tray and went to get his drink.

"You getting too familiar with this boy. You fucking him?" he said as he brought a fork full of rice and stew chicken to his mouth.

"No, Daddy." She looked down and pushed the lie through her lips as quickly as possible.

"I don't believe you! If you fuck around and get pregnant, you outta this muthafucka. You need to be trying to change the curse yo sorry ass mother left on you."

"I'ma make you proud of me, Daddy," she said meekly.

"I doubt that," he snorted taking another spoon full of food. He chewed slowly and stared at her like he could see physical evidence of her indiscretion.

Raven stood frozen in place wondering if it would be a mistake for Flint to come inside when he arrived. Her dad could be a real asshole and Flint was a ticking time bomb. She knew things could get ugly. The doorbell rang and she damned near jumped out of her skin.

"Well, get the door. I need to see why yo ass get wet every time the phone ring."

Raven unglued her feet from the spot and headed to the door.

"Hey babe," she said. Her smile caused her one dimple to dig deep into her cheek.

"What's up, ma?" Flint responded leaning in and kissing her forehead.

"I want you to meet my Daddy. He's in the family room," she whispered as she tried to fight the butterflies in her stomach.

"Relax," he said smoothly as he walked off.

She locked the door and followed close behind.

"Daddy, this is Flint. Flint this is my dad, Glen." Raven made the introduction as she tried to use Flint as a shield.

"Don't hide. Let me see your face while I question this young man," her father ordered as he raised his glass to his lips.

Flint tightened his fist close to his leg in an effort to calm his nerves. He could already see shit was about to get real.

"You can be seated," Glen said as he reached over and grabbed a cigarette and lighter from the end table next to his chair.

Flint took a seat on the edge of the couch and sat up looking her father right in the eyes.

"So what are your intentions towards my daughter?" he asked, putting fire to his cigarette and inhaling deeply.

"I care about her and I plan on spending as much time with her as she will allow and show her just how much she means to me," he said, making sure to hold firm eye contact.

"And what do you do with that time? You fucking my daughter?"

"Raven, go wait in the car," Flint said and handed her the keys.

"You better not move," her father ordered. If it wasn't for the faint sound of the television Raven's heart would have been the loudest thing in the room.

"This is a man to man talk." Flint gave her father a hard stare.

His mind flashed back to that night in the hotel and at that moment he knew exactly why she was so afraid to be with him. He got sick at the mere thought. He decided that this would be the last night her father would terrorize or intimidate her.

Raven looked at her dad then back at Flint. Flint looked up at her and smiled.

"I'll be right out," he said. His words were tender but he had a look of death in his eyes.

Raven felt her hands shake as she processed the idea of walking out against her father's orders. Just as she was about to crack under the pressure she inhaled deeply and went with her gut.

"See you later, Daddy," she mumbled and turned as quickly as she could to exit the house.

Flint waited until he heard the door close then dropped the smile from his face. He gave her dad the look that said *I'll kill you in this muthafucka.*

"Let me tell you something, you sorry muthafucka. With all due respect, all that right there belongs to me now. She don't owe you shit and neither do I. Out of respect for her I'ma let you breathe. However, if you ever come out your mouth to me like that again, I'll blow your fucking head off." With those words, Flint rose to his feet.

"Is that what you think?" Glen fought through the fear to utter a few last words.

"Nah, nigga, that's what I know. Engrave that shit in the front of your mind," he spat as he turned to leave the room.

"You can have the bitch. I believe she served her purpose," he said and chuckled as he heard the door slam.

"She'll be back," Glen yelled.

Glen took a few more hits on his cigarette as the threat sunk in. Up to that point, he'd had full control over his daughter. Now, he knew he needed to do something to break the hold that Flint now had on her. He knew that with a little salt in the game any nigga could be broken.

CHAPTER 18

Unbreakable

Over the next month, everything changed.

Raven moved in with Flint. The day she told her father that she was moving out would remain etched in her mind forever. Flint had really shown his gangster that evening. Up against another man, Glen folded like a lawn chair.

Breonni and Long were still tight but, for some reason she still didn't understand, he hadn't hit that yet.

Jovanna continued to try to have a relationship with Shawn, but he still treated her like shit.

Katina and Naseem seemed to be two happy love birds but Katina was so caught up with Naseem that she missed the deadline for her scholarship. She had to push her plans to start school back to spring semester. Her parents were livid. In order to escape the pressure at home, she had recently moved in with Naseem.

The girls were so into their relationships that they had been neglecting the friendship. They decided to have a girl's night and they were about to turn all the way up.

"You sure you wanna go to New York?" Jovonna asked. She stood in the mirror in Raven's bedroom putting on lipstick.

"Yes, we do. And, don't start that scary shit," Breonni said pulling her shirt over her head. "We didn't do shit for our birthdays. We been all up under these niggas but tonight we gonna have some fun," she said doing a little dance.

Katina sat on the bed and watched as they moved around Raven and Flint's room getting dressed and passing blunts. She was conflicted about the whole idea. Naseem had left instructions for her to stay in the house but, being the mother hen of the group, she did not want them going out without somebody with some sense in the mix.

"Why you so quiet, Tina?" Raven asked as she took a seat next to her.

"No reason. I'm just watching y'all." She forced a smile.

"Stop kissing her ass, Rav. She likes to bring rain to a nice sunny day," Breonni said walking over to them. "Here, hit this and relax." Breonni put the blunt in front of her face.

"I don't want that!" Katina scrunched up her face and pushed Breonni's hand away.

"Oh, that's right. Say no to drugs," Breonni joked. They all chuckled.

"Whatever. I need my lungs. Thank you very much." Katina waved her hand to block the smoke Breonni blew in her direction.

"Leave Tina alone. One of us gotta be clear headed," Jovanna said as she put on her jewelry.

"We ready?" Raven asked looking everyone over.

Breonni turned to look at her girls. They all had on tight, dark blue jeans with a tank and blazer and three inch heels. "We look like a goddamn singing group," she said looking them up and down.

When they realized it they all erupted in laughter. "Well, bitch, I'm Beyonce," Raven said doing a little booty shake.

"We all gonna be Ike and Tina when they find out we dipped off," Jovanna added.

"Oh shit," Raven said chuckling as they grabbed their purses and went out the door. Katina just smiled as she thought about the reality of Jovanna's statement.

On the ride over the music was jumping and they sang and bopped in their seats ready for the night. When Raven pulled up to the Lion's Den all of their eyes were doing flips trying to keep up with all the action.

"This is a Motorcycle club?" Katina asked as she started to get a little sick to her stomach.

"It's not just for motorcycles. It has dance floors and gambling. My hair stylist said this place is official," Raven answered as she pulled Flint's BMW up to the gate.

"I'm ready," Breonni said as her eyes wandered over all the ballers in attendance. "These niggas caked up," she added as Raven paid and pushed on through the gate.

Katina looked back as the doors shut. It felt like her fate was sealed. Raven pulled next to a black Benz with weed smoke coming out all the windows and felt like she was home.

The four of them jumped out of the car. Breonni threw her jacket in the back seat and each one of them followed suit except Katina. She felt like raw meat amongst wolves.

Katina walked close to Jovonna. They were damned near joined at the hip.

"Relax, mama. We just gonna dance for a little while, then be out." Jovanna tried to ease Katina's mind.

"You're right. Let me try to enjoy myself." Katina took a breath and they headed to the elevator.

When they got to the main dance floor, Breonni went into rare form. She hit the bar and ordered a few drinks for Raven, JoJo, and her. Katina stood next to them looking at all the action. Females were half dressed in leather and high heels and the men where all over them. It was like a big happy orgy. Flashing lights and loud music consumed the room as bodies contorted on the dance floor.

"To us," Breonni said and raised her glass. The women touched theirs with hers and began throwing drinks back.

After they finished their drinks, they hit the dance floor. It was on. They lined up back to back and started getting it in. After a few moves they soon had partners. They got in the groove with a few guys and threw their inhibitions out the window. It was officially a party.

* * * * *

"So, we good?" Naseem asked as he collected the product and placed it in the bags.

The bond between Baseem and Naseem still had cracks, but business was booming so regardless of the small snag Baseem had to respect Naseem's hustle.

Baseem looked over at Chucky who was putting the last stack in the money machine. When he nodded to the count being on point Baseem responded, "Yeah, we straight."

"A'ight, then. I'll see you in two weeks," Naseem

announced as he stood up. When he looked over Baseem's shoulder at the monitors his eyes lowered and his brow creased as his gaze settled on the middle of the dance floor.

"What the fuck?" he said as his nostrils flared.

"What you see?" Long asked as he stood to see what had Naseem alarmed.

"They must be out of their muthafuckin' mind," Long remarked as he reached into his pocket and called Breonni's phone. He watched her look at her phone and send the call to voice mail. "Oh shit she sent me to the machine."

"That's your girl, Nas. She seems to be having fun," Baseem teased as he watched one of his crew members trying to push up on her.

"I'll hit you later," Naseem said as he headed to the door with Long and Flint on his heels.

"Little mama 'bout to get fucked up," Baseem predicted as he watched Naseem move through the crowd.

"If I had pussy like that waiting on me, she would be home naked in my bed waiting for me to come through the door." Chucky grinned.

"He don't know what to do with a woman yet. I taught him a lot but he missed that lesson," Baseem said as he focused his eyes on the action that was taking place. "Go down there before shit get outta hand. You see she dancing with Stevo. You know that nigga crazy than a muthafucka," he ordered. Chucky headed out.

"What the fuck is you doing here?" Naseem's voice boomed damn near as loud as the music.

When Katina looked up she almost pissed her pants. She wanted to answer but her words got stuck in her throat.

"We—I—."

Naseem stared down at her with heat coming from his eyes.

"How the fuck y'all get here?" Flint asked giving Raven the same cold hard stare.

"I drove your BMW, baby," she answered in a tiny voice. Flint sighed and shook his head.

Beside him, Naseem was boiling. "Let's go," Naseem said taking Katina by the wrist.

"Hold up. They having fun," Stevo interrupted stepping into their path.

Naseem moved Katina behind him.

"Mind your muthafuckin' business," he barked.

Flint and Long lined up next to him and several dudes standing close to them turned around and stood next to Stevo.

"Nigga, you make me mind my fuckin' business," Stevo said resting his hand in his jacket.

Breonni bravely stepped between them. "This shit ain't necessary," she cried.

"Bre, get yo ass out the way." Long grabbed her arm and pulled her to the side.

The crowd moved back when Naseem and Stevo stepped nose to nose.

Before another word was said, Chucky was at Stevo's side whispering something in his ear. Stevo looked up towards the cameras and nodded his understanding. "My bad, young un'. I didn't know you were family. Let's go, my niggas," he said to his boys. They moved away giving Naseem and his crew dirty looks as they walked off.

"Go ahead and get your girls up outta here. This ain't

no play ground," Chucky spat as he, too, turned to walk away.

Naseem was on fire. He looked down at Katina. No words were needed, she heard him loud and clear. She headed towards the elevator walking as if her life depended on it. Breonni was pissed and embarrassed. She stomped right behind her. Jovonna and Raven put pep in their steps as they felt the heat from Flint's eyes scorching their backs.

When Flint and Long met at Naseem's truck, he had to regroup.

"Long, you take the product in your car so me and Flint can make sure they get home safely," he instructed. He cut his eyes at the girls and hardened his stare.

"Y'all ride with Flint. Katina, come get in my truck," he ordered leaving no room for negotiation.

Jovanna and Breonni climbed into Flint's back seat; Breonni sat with her arms folded across her chest and her mouth a tight line. Raven slid into the front seat at the same time as Flint, but dared not even look in his direction.

Katina got in the front seat of her man's whip and stared straight ahead as she fastened her seat belt. As they pulled out of the parking spot she said softly. "I'm sorry."

Naseem didn't respond. He drove in silence. He did not trust his tongue. He whipped through the streets and headed toward the tunnel thinking about that nigga in the club who had just stepped into his crosshairs.

Naseem pulled into his parking space still trying to cool off from what happened.

Katina fidgeted with her purse in anticipation of what Naseem was going to say to her when they got in the house.

They exited the vehicle and headed in the building. Naseem remained quiet all the way to the apartment door. Once inside he went straight to his room grabbed a few things and prepared to leave the apartment.

"You're going out?" Katina asked as the weight of the evening consumed her emotions.

"Yeah, I got shit to take care of," Naseem said coldly continuing to the door. Tonight Katina would get her first lesson on what happens when she disobeyed him.

"Naseem, please don't leave," she pleaded walking behind him.

"Lock the door. I'll see you in a couple of days," Naseem remarked allowing the door to slam behind him.

Katina locked the door then rested her hands against it as water rose in her eyes. When she turned to the living room regret rushed through her body. She took off her jacket threw it on the floor, plopped down on the couch and began to cry.

Naseem stayed away from the house for the rest of the weekend as he processed what steps he needed to make next. The way things had shifted the chances of him leaving the house and coming back safe was getting slimmer. Naseem didn't just have a concern for his safety he now had to worry about Katina. He had to make her understand that this shit was not a game before she put them both in danger.

Late Monday evening, Naseem walked into the apartment and was met by Katina's beautiful face. She was uncertain of his mood and worried about what would come out of his mouth. She stood in the middle of the kitchen waiting for him to make the first move.

"We need to talk."

Naseem took Katina by the hand and led her to the living room. Katina followed him with worry in her heart that showed on her face. She took a seat next to him on the couch and stared down at the floor.

Naseem held her hand in his and spoke bluntly, "I'm into some things that I don't want to involve you in. I am trying to do everything in my power to keep this away from you, but shit like you did the other night makes my job harder."

Katina feared for the worst was about to come out his mouth.

"You're not leaving me are you?"

"Nah, ma. Nothing like that. I just want to keep you safe. When you are into what I'm into people can use what you love to hurt you."

"I understand," She said and placed her hand on his leg.

Naseem put his hand on top of hers and stared into her eyes.

"I hope you do because muthafuckas can't be trusted. You can't go running the streets anyplace at any time because muthafuckas are always plotting. I trust one person and that's Long. I trust him with my life. If anything ever happens to me he can look out for you."

A single tear came down Katina's face when she thought about the danger she could have put them in.

"Don't cry, ma. It's all good." Naseem said and flashed a reassuring smile. "The main thing I need you to do is not add to the problem. When I tell you stay home it's not so I can run shit. These niggas don't respect nothing. That shit you and your girls pulled the other night could have gotten deadly. Don't do that shit no more." It was a loving, but stern, warning.

"I promise. It won't happen again."

He reached up and wiped the tears away from her face. "We have to move differently now. I can't live with the idea that I would be the cause of something happening to you."

He looked into her eyes then leaned in and hugged her tightly. Katina climbed into Naseem's lap.

"I need to feel you," she purred kissing him lightly on the lips.

"You act like you missed me."

"I always miss you. I'm sorry."

She kissed him again slipping her tongue into his mouth. His soldier stood up. He was getting ready to put in work.

"Let me strap up," he said.

"No. I want to feel all of you," she cooed as she went for his zipper. Katina ground her pelvis against him to bring his soldier to a full salute.

Naseem was uncertain. Still, he wasn't going to argue about getting to feel all that wet raw. He had been trying to be careful to avoid pregnancy but Katina was not taking no for an answer. Naseem released the beast and held it firmly in his hand.

"You want it. Take it," he offered lustfully.

Katina slithered down Naseem's body and let out a sexy moan as she began to handle that dick like a pro.

Naseem laid his head back and closed his eyes as he guided her waist. Within minutes she was slippery wet and her muscles were tightening with every bounce. She picked up speed making him hit her spot just right. Tonight she wanted more than sex, she wanted him to give her a very special part of him.

"I'm coming, Nas," she mumbled in his ear and bit into his neck.

Her tightness along with the wet slip and slide action was bringing him to release sooner than he wanted to. He was trying to let her get hers so he could pull out but his battle with control was about to come to an end.

"Ummmm, let me pull out. I'm about to come."

"I said I want all of you."

Katina gripped the back of the couch with both hands and kept on riding.

All Naseem could do was enjoy. When Katina started to talk to him, he just closed his eyes and held her tightly.

"I will always love you. You are my king and I will always be here for you," professed Katina.

Naseem released a few moans of pleasure and pumped up into her as if his life depended on it. She bounced up and down as her hips rotated to the beat of her heart. Her body tensed up as she began to come once more.

"Open your eyes," she commanded.

Naseem opened them slowly and he tried to focus. When their eyes locked, she fought hard to hold back the tears. She kept sliding up and down slowly allowing her slippery lips to say the words her mouth could not.

"Kiss me," she cooed.

Naseem gave her some tongue. Katina sucked on it passionately then pulled back and looked into her man's eyes.

"Baby, always be honest with me and I will love you forever."

"I got you, ma," he said with sincerity as he began to release deep inside her hot beckoning womb.

Katina held herself in place to assure she had every drop. There was more than love between them. There was an unbreakable bond that they vowed to uphold at all cost. The streets had his commitments but Katina had his heart. Naseem wanted to make sure the streets never came to her. But the way things were moving he feared that it was just a matter of time before the shit he tried to hold back caught up to them.

CHAPTER 19

Deception

"Hold your hands steady," Long instructed.

He stood behind Breonni with his hands on top of hers with the gun firmly in her grip. He had been training her to handle different weapons for the past few nights. She was good with the small caliber guns but she needed more practice with the big Glock's and German Lugers. He wanted her to be able to handle every weapon in his stash.

"I'm trying. This shit heavy," she said as she tried to lock her eyes on the target and hold the Glock .50 steady.

"You can do it. Stop acting like a girl and bust this shit," he teased. "Just relax and breathe and grip the handle tight."

"Get your dick off of my ass so I can concentrate," she joked.

"That is the incentive."

He moved his hands down and placed them around her waist.

"Hit that target, baby."

Breonni gripped the handle, closed one eye, and focused on the three bottles he had set up. She squeezed the trigger three times rapidly in succession hitting two of the bottles and leaving one behind. The roar echoed through the darkness of Weequahic Park.

"That's what the fuck I'm talking about! That's how I want you to lay a muthafucka down!"

"They gonna be in trouble coming for us," She said as she turned the gun over in her hand.

"Look at you," Long grinned proudly as he reached for the gun. "Gimme this shit before you bust both of us."

"You know you love it when I bust you off."

Breonni gave him that hungry look that let him know he had something to look forward to later.

"Come on, l'il mama. We gotta pick up Shawn and Jovonna," Long said tucking the guns in a black backpack within a secret compartment in the trunk.

Breonni hopped in the front seat and fastened her seat belt.

When they pulled in front of Shawn's house, Long called his cell to tell them to come out.

"This nigga always slow as hell," Long said aloud as he tried to remain calm. If it wasn't for Breonni wanting to see her girl he would have pulled off.

After about fifteen minutes, they came out with Jovanna tagging far behind Shawn like a little kid on punishment. Breonni watched her body language as she moved to the backseat.

"What's up, Diva?" Breonni said giving her girl a warm greeting.

"What's up Shawn?" she asked although she really

didn't give a fuck.

"Hey, mama," Jovonna said. She sounded slightly defeated.

"Hey, Bre," Shawn said as he settled in his seat.

Breonni's lips got tight as she tried to bite her tongue. Breonni's nostrils flared and her mind raced. Long shook his head in an attempt to calm her down.

Breonni looked back at Shawn who was gazing out the window trying to avoid eye contact. She reached over and turned up the music then turned around in her seat. She was ready to blow.

The drive was uncomfortably silent. As soon as they reached the restaurant, Breonni grabbed her girl by the hand and damned near dragged her into the bathroom. Long watched them leave.

"What's up with your girl?" Long asked.

"Ain't shit wrong with her. She just spoiled," Shawn said. It was clear he didn't want to answer any more questions.

"Yeah, a'ight."

Long turned to the hostess to reserve their table.

Inside the bathroom, Breonni questioned Jovanna.

"What the fuck is wrong with you? Is that nigga hitting you?"

"No, Bre," she replied. Tears began to run down her face.

"What's the matter?" Breonni took her by the hand and led her to the paper towel dispenser.

Jovanna took a minute to try to get her thoughts together. Through tears and sniffles she began to tell all.

"He made me get an abortion yesterday. Right before y'all picked me up he told me that he has another baby on the way and he couldn't have two."

"That muthafucka," Breonni turned to the door.

"Bre, no. You're gonna make it worse."

Jovanna grabbed Breonni by the arm to pull her back.

"Fuck that. That nigga foul."

"It's okay. Don't worry. I got it."

"No, the fuck it ain't. Why the next bitch worthy to have his baby and you ain't? You over that niggas house every day, damn near like you his wife and he fucking a bitch on the side and she get to have his baby. Where the fuck they do that at?" Breonni bristled.

The words came off her tongue so hot it felt like it was on fire. Jovonna didn't have a reply. She had been wondering the same thing.

"Why didn't you tell us you were pregnant?" Breonni asked.

"I was scared. When y'all asked if we had sex the night of prom I lied."

She looked down feeling ashamed.

"He pulled back from me and, out of fear of losing him, I gave in a few days later. I got pregnant that same night," she confessed in a low tone.

"JoJo, you could have told us. That is what we are here for, ma," Breonni said.

"Bre, please, promise me you won't say anything. I don't need this right now," she pleaded.

"You don't need that shit he putting you through!"

"Bre, please. I know he loves me. It was the best thing to do. Promise me you won't say anything."

Breonni stood still. She focused her energy on calming down. She wanted to go out there and knock Shawn's head

TAINTED

off his shoulders. That bitch ass muthafucka had broken her girl. For her girl's sake, she would bite her tongue but somehow someway his punk ass was going to pay.

Looking into Jovonna's eyes she mumbled through tight lips. "You have my word."

Breonni took Jovanna into her arms and hugged her tightly. After a few minutes, they washed their faces, applied fresh makeup and headed out of the bathroom. Breonni struggled to control her emotions.

Forcing a smile, she said, "Did y'all order drinks?"

"Yo ass ain't drinking," Long said meeting eyes with hers looking for confirmation that everything was fine.

"Just one, pleeease. I need it," she said, putting her hands together then giving him a big smile.

"You alright?" he asked.

"Yeah, I'm good," she half-lied and nudged his foot under the table.

Long took that to mean that she would tell him the truth later. Drinking was not her thing which further confirmed that shit was not right.

Dinner was miserable. The four of them ate and tried to keep the conversation civil but the mood was ruined. Jovanna was quiet with an occasional smile to mask her pain. Shawn's eyes looked empty and he avoided eye contact with Breonni who was shooting him daggers ever so often. After diner they dropped Shawn and Jovonna off. Breonni wasted no time speaking her mind about Long's punk ass friend.

"Baby let me tell you about your bitch ass boy," she began.

Breonni didn't stop talking until she let it all out.

Long drove around town to allow her time to vent. When she stopped to take a breath, he calmly said his piece.

"Look, ya girl gotta make her own decisions. Just be there for her but don't try to stop that shit because she will fuck around and turn on you," he advised as he pulled up in front of Breonni's building.

"I understand, but the shit don't sit well with me," she said. Breonni propped her elbow on the window. She was still wrestling with the anger that was boiling in her belly.

"Baby, let it go. She ain't gonna stop fucking with him so you just gotta be a good friend and hopefully everything will pan out."

"Ya boy is a bitch ass nigga and I ain't got nothing for him so please keep me away from him," she stated as she got out the car.

"You still love me, right?" Long joked as she marched up the stairs and into the building. She slammed the door on her way in.

Long knew the shit was foul but that was Shawn's business. He had no intention of getting involved.

Breonni went straight to the bathroom and hopped into the shower. A few minutes later, she pulled on her pajamas and climbed into bed with murder on her mind. Shawn had just made it to the top of her shit list. All he needed was to make one more wrong move and she was going to erase all of Jovanna's problems. Long had taught the wrong bitch how to handle a gun.

CHAPTER 20

I Got Your Back

"Yo, my nigga, put that money where your mouth is," Long yelled out shaking the dice in his hand ready to shoot them against the wall.

"Nigga, stop popping shit and swing them bitches," Flint said waiting to see what fate the black and white would reveal.

Everyone stood back as Long rolled the dice. When they came to a stop they landed on seven. "Pay me nigga, put my shit on floor and back the fuck up," he spat, picking up the dice ready to break all them niggas pockets.

"Fuck you, nigga," Flint slurred. He removed the blunt from his mouth and laid his money next to Long's boot.

"That's what all sorry ass losers say," Long spat as he prepared to roll again.

When the dice again hit seven, niggas started sweating. They were up to a thousand dollars a roll and he had just hit five in a row.

"Y'all muthafuckas 'bout to buy me another car," he joked as he picked up his winnings and prepared to go in for the kill.

Long threw the dice one more time and came up with seven again.

"Let me see them punk ass dice," Geronimo yelled out pulling his gun from his waist. "Who brought them muthafuckas up in here? Confess so I can let my bitch speak 'cause my pockets about to start a war in this bitch."

The room erupted in laughter.

"Yo ass crazy as hell," Naseem slapped hands with Geronimo.

"Nah, you brought this lucky ass nigga up in here. You getting it first," he chuckled as he peeled another thousand off his knot.

"Thank you for your support," Long said as he collected his money.

As he organized the bills, the phone on his hip started to vibrate. He looked down at the number and realized it was Hennessey. He had missed his call twice. He quickly stepped to the side to take the call.

"Yeah, answer the phone. Maybe it will be some bad ass luck on the other end and we can get some of that tight fist you got over there," Fuqaun yelled out as Long turned.

"What's up, nigga?" Long said into the phone as he motioned for the little cutie they had serving drinks to pour him something nice.

"I usually wouldn't bother you. I know what night it is. But I'm sitting across from Breonni's building and she is sitting out here on the cold concrete looking shocked as hell."

Long looked at his watch. It was 2:45 A.M. *What the fuck is wrong with her?*

"Do me a favor. Get little mama and put her in your car. I'm on my way."

"I got you," Hennessey said.

Long took his drink to the head, slammed the glass on the counter, and turned back to the crew.

"I'ma get at y'all niggas later," he said and began slapping hands.

"You good, my nigga?" Naseem looked on with curiosity.

"Yeah, I'm straight. I gotta go handle something real quick. I'll holla at you later today."

"A'ight," Naseem said. He didn't know what was up but he knew that shit had to be serious if he was leaving money to go chase it.

"Ain't this a bitch? You gonna take a nigga lunch money and bounce," Geronimo griped slapping hands with Long.

"You know what they say. Hit the pussy until you nut. Pull out, shake it, then roll." He bumped fists with Geronimo and continued, "I get up."

Long nodded and headed towards the door.

"A'ight, you my nigga if he don't get no bigger. And, if you get any bigger, you'll just be my bigger nigga," Geronimo joked. "Now I gotta play with you broke muthafuckas roll that shit," he continued with his mind also on his boy's sudden change of attitude.

Long and he went way back, like freeze tag and hop scotch.

Long pushed on, hopped into his car and went to pick up Breonni.

On Day Street, things were still moving like it was the middle of the day. He parked and jumped out of his ride and walked over to Hennessey's truck. When Breonni saw him coming, her heart warmed up replacing the pain and disappointment of the last few hours.

"What's up?" Long asked, reaching in the window and giving Hennessey a pound.

"Ain't shit."

He said to Breonni, "Come on, little mama."

"Thanks, Henney. I'll catch up with you later."

"Anytime."

Hennessey hit the lock and Long opened the door so Breonni could climb out of the back seat. Breonni stared at the cracks in the black tar not wanting to make eye contact with Long.

"You straight?" he asked.

He lifted her chin to see her face. The bruise under her left eye filled him with rage.

"Who put their fucking hands on you?" He demanded to know.

"It's okay. Let's just leave," Breonni pleaded taking him by the hand.

She could see murder in his bloodshot eyes.

"I'm not asking you twice," he said in a voice as hard as the steel in his waist.

Breonni swallowed and forced out the name, "Mike."

Her voice was as low as an ant's piss on cotton.

"Who?"

Breonni repeated the name louder this time. Long knitted his brow and said, "Wait right here."

He hit the alarm on his car and opened the door.

"Where you going?" she asked as she slid into the seat.

Long didn't answer. He looked over at Henney, nodded, and then hit the alarm locking her inside.

Henney jumped out of his truck, slammed the door and stepped hard as he followed Long into the building. They ran up the four flights of steps to Breonni's apartment. Long pulled out his nine and banged on the door. Hennessey stood watch at the end of the hall with his gat firmly in his hand. After a few more hard knocks the door opened only the distance the chain would allow.

"Why the fuck you knocking on this door like that, nigga?" Breonni's brother barked through the crack.

Long kicked the door open sending it crashing into the wall and knocking Mike onto the floor. He jumped on top of the nigga and began beating him in the head and face with his gun.

Mike struggled beneath him for a while then just lay still. Long put the gun into his mouth and stared down into his eyes.

"If you ever put your hands on her again, I'ma give you one more hole in your head. Am I clear?"

Mike slightly nodded. Blood ran from his mouth, nose, and several gashes on his forehead. Long stood up, tore a piece of Mike's shirt, and used it to clean the blood from his gun.

"Where is her room?"

Mike lifted his shaky hand and pointed over his head. Long stepped over him kicking him as he moved toward the hallway. When Mike looked up again through his busted eye, he saw Hennessey standing in the doorway with his gun drawn.

Long walked into Breonni's room, looked around, and then grabbed her two Gucci duffle bags from the closet. He filled them with a few outfits and all her jewelry from the dresser, and then he was out.

Stepping back over Mike's body, he spat a few more words, "Remember what I told you. And, you ain't see neither one of us, nigga. With your punk ass."

Long and Hennessy left the apartment and headed back to the car. Long popped the trunk and threw the bags inside. Hennessey and he hit fists and peeled out. Breonni cracked a small smile. She knew that Long had love for her but she wasn't sure how much until she saw the blood on his shirt and gun in his hand. She remained silent the whole ride. She didn't want to say anything that would mess up her moment.

When they arrived at his apartment he grabbed her bags from the trunk and took her inside. When he hit the lights, she was pleasantly surprised. Everything was perfectly in place. The decor of the living room consisted of different shades of dark red. The couch, love seat, and chairs were deep red with big black pillows. Gold and glass coffee and end tables set off the deep green, red and black print of the plush area rug that lay underneath. This was not the type of apartment she would have thought a hood dude would have. In the few months they had been hanging out, he would always run in and out the house. She had to admit the circumstances of being there weren't great but the timing was just right.

"Why you looking around like you thought I was living in an empty room with an air mattress and piss bucket?" Long joked as he headed down the hall to the guest bedroom. He hit the light and placed her bags in the closet.

"You can make yourself at home. I grabbed what I thought you needed. I'll take you to get some things tomorrow. Towels and wash cloths are in the bathroom," he said, pulling his shirt over his head.

Breonni's eyes moved over his chest and down his abs. Her mind began to wonder how good he would feel with all that power covering her small frame.

"Come take a shower with me," he said, walking down the hall towards the bathroom.

Breonni was beyond excited. She walked behind him wearing a big smile on her face. When she entered the bathroom, he was already out of his clothes and adjusting the water.

Breonni eyed every part of his body. As he ran the cloth over his skin, her body heated up like an oven.

"What happened between you and your brother?" he asked as he took the cloth from her hands and began to glide it over her arms neck and chest.

"He is always like that. My family is fucked up. My mom stay at the bar. I think I had seen my father twice and my brother is the worst. Instead of protecting me he abuses me verbally or physically every chance he get," she paused then went on. "Ever since I was little I had been fighting to be free."

Long turned her around and began to ease the soapy cloth over her neck and back.

"Don't worry, ma. You got me. I'ma always make sure you're straight," he vowed.

Long dropped the cloth to the shower floor and rubbed his soapy hands over her butt. Her revelation was not one he hadn't heard before. Breonni had masked her pain well. Tonight was the first time he saw that she was an injured soul. Long had been trying to avoid being her first. Those types of feelings came with big responsibility. Now, with all she was feeling tonight, he wanted to give her some type of comfort.

The warm water cascaded over them. Long turned her to face him and wrapped her in his arms. Her soft breasts rested against his chest.

"I know you're not ready for all that comes with my big world but I'ma give you a sample," he said. His deep voice caressed her ears causing a rush of wetness between her thighs.

Long wrapped one arm around her waist and cuffed her leg with the other flipping her upside down. Her knees rested on his shoulder and his hard dick stared her in the face. He gripped his arms tight around her back and began gliding his tongue across her clit.

Soft whispers of pleasure passed her lips as he sucked and kissed her throbbing clit. Breonni took his long thick pipe in her hand and pushed him to the back of her throat.

Long let out deep grunts between running his tongue between her soft wet lips. Breonni moved her head back and forth savoring his flavor. She grabbed his ass and tightened her jaws as she felt her juices begin to flow. Long's dick hardened in her mouth as her sexy moans and jaw-lock caused his knees to wobble.

Simultaneously, they released into each other's mouths and licked and swallowed the sweet release. Long held her tightly for a few more seconds allowing his lips and tongue to enjoy the reward her pussy had just given him.

Breonni wouldn't be outdone. She continued to suck until she made sure to swallow everything he offered. As she moved her head away, she kissed the tip as it passed her lips.

Long gently released her and positioned her back on her feet. Drunk with pleasure and wobbly on her feet, Breonni rested against his chest waiting to see what else he had in store. She took his semi erect dick into her hands and played in the little bit of cum she'd left behind.

"You ain't ready for this dick yet. This right here is for big girls," he said with low eyes as she stroked her hand up and down his length.

"I'm not a big girl?" she cooed, trying to bring him back to life.

"Not yet. But when it's time, I'ma have fun making you one," he replied. His deep voice caused her coochie to tingle.

"Let's rinse off and get some rest. We had a long day. Let me taste that tongue."

He put his tongue deep into her mouth. His soulful kiss stole her breath. Breonni savored the passion between them. Afterward, they washed each other's bodies tenderly.

Long lotioned his body, threw on some boxers, and climbed between the sheets of his bed. Breonni moved around the spare room trying to familiarize herself with the layout. She scented her skin and dressed in an oversized tank top. Then, she slowly crept down the hall to where Long lay peacefully. She tip-toed to the side of the bed and stared at him. Long felt Breonni breathing down on him like a thief in the night.

"What's up, ma?" he mumbled opening his lids.

"Can I please sleep in here with you?" she asked with her bottom lip poked out.

Long stared at her then looked at the clock on his nightstand. It was 4:45 A.M. and her sexy eyes were pleading from the other side of the bed.

"Come on but take yo ass to sleep. No footsies."

He pulled the covers back. Breonni jumped in and snuggled next to him.

"Thank you, Long." she laid her head on his chest.

"You know I got your back, ma. Now, hush so I can get some sleep."

Breonni dared not say another word. She closed her eyes and fell further into heaven. Within seconds, she was fast asleep. Long looked down at Breonni and wondered what he had gotten himself into. He loved her but he was not ready for a relationship. The last thing he wanted was to cause Breonni more pain.

CHAPTER 21

The Next Level

The next afternoon Long got up, showered, got dressed and prepared to leave the house. Breonni sat in his bed and watched as he tucked his gun, and gathered stacks of money from his drawer and placed them in a small black bag and zipped it closed.

"You gonna be straight here all day?"

"I thought we were going shopping," she announced, feeling a little deflated.

"Nah, we can do that tomorrow. I gotta go take care of something. I got mad food so you should be good. There's a spare set of keys and seven hundred dollars in the kitchen drawer if you have to leave out to get something, but I prefer that you stay put."

"I won't leave the house," she said, crawling to the end of the bed and rising to her knees. Breonni motioned with her finger for him to come over to her.

Long positioned himself right in front of her. Breonni stood up and took his face into her hands. "I'ma miss you while you're gone," she said placing her lips on his.

Long let her have her pleasure then said, "Be good."

He pulled away from her and headed to the door. Breonni plopped back onto the bed and crossed her legs. To an outsider, it would have appeared that she had won her prize but, in her heart, she knew she was living a lie.

Breonni stayed in the house for the next three days. Long was in and out but it was like she lived there alone. The boredom was borderline depressing. She flipped through a few TV channels then called up Katina and the girls. They agreed to meet at Katina's house.

Breonni got dressed. On the way to Katina's, she stopped at the mall where she picked up a pair jeans and a t-shirt from Macy's, a pair of sneakers, and several thongs from Victoria Secrets. Then, she caught a cab to Katina's house.

"Hey Bre," Katina said as she opened the door.

"What's up, Boo?" Breonni asked, "Where is the crew?"

"Girl, you know you can't get Jovonna out of Shawn's face and Flint told Raven to stay in the house," she reported shaking her head as she closed the door.

"These bitches all wifed up. Y'all getting me depressed," Breonni spat as she walked into the living room. "Don't make no damned sense."

Katina chuckled.

"Look at you, all glowing and shit," Breonni complimented as she placed her hand on Katina's stomach.

"Was Naseem happy? How far are you?" she asked.

"Only two months but, yes, he is very happy."

The women sat on the couch to catch each other up on the latest.

"So, did you tell your parents yet?" Breonni asked. She reached into her purse, pulled out two Snicker bars, and passed one to Katina.

"Awww, thanks, Bre,"

Katina started opening the candy and thought about her answer.

"When I told my mom, she was a little upset because of my plans for school but I know she will support me. I can't tell my dad. He is going to flip all the way out. We haven't really spoke since I moved out."

"Well, bitch, you better say something because your ass getting big fast," Breonni said as she smacked away on her chocolate treat.

"You don't have to rub it in. My jeans are all tight on my booty." She turned to the side and looked at it before continuing. "But, never mind my issues. What is going on with you and Long?"

"Girl, don't get me started with that nigga. He got a bitch head fucked up."

"You gave him some?" Katina's eyes got wide.

"Girl that nigga a big ass tease. Got me ready to rape his ass."

Katina burst out laughing. "Why you think he holding out?"

"I don't know. If it's another bitch, she's well hidden because I live at his house and I'm with him all the time. I just don't know, Tina."

"Well, maybe he just respects you enough to wait until he feels y'all are ready."

"Fuck that! He can respect me in the morning after he make me feel that steel. I want that nigga to show me some hateful dick."

"You so stupid!" Katina screamed laughing at the thought.

"Sheeit. I ain't playing, I don't even know why I'm over here in your little love nest. This shit got me feeling all Lucy and Ricky Ricardo," Breonni laughed.

Just as they were changing the subject, the front door opened and slammed shut.

"What y'all got going on up in here?" Naseem asked walking over to Katina and kissing her on the lips.

"Nothing. Just chillin'," Katina responded.

Breonni looked up and saw Long in the doorway. When their eyes met, images of their last time together replayed in her mind.

"What's up, little mama?" he asked as he walked over to the couch.

"Nothing much," Breonni responded in a slightly low voice.

Katina smiled at the look of her girl caught up in the love. Breonni acted tough but when Long came into the room she became shy. Katina could feel the attraction between them. She shook her head thinking about what Bre had just shared.

"What you about to do?" Naseem asked as he headed to the bedroom.

"Why? You need something?" Katina got up and followed him, allowing Breonni a minute alone with Long.

"I always need something," he said with a sneaky grin.

"Because you're spoiled," Katina smiled back as they entered the room and shut the door.

Long sat beside her and looked in the bags at her feet.

"I see you been out spending my money."

"Yeah, is that problem?" Breonni tipped her head to the side.

"Nah, you can have whatever I got."

"I can't tell," she shot back crossing her arms over her chest.

"Keep being grown. You gonna wish you were still a little girl fucking with me."

"Whatever. With your scary ass," she said turning away from him.

"Stop pouting and let me taste your lips," he said pulling her to him.

Breonni gave in allowing him to tongue her down. When she came up for air, he looked in her eyes and said, "Don't worry. I got you."

"I know."

"Go to the house. I got some shit to do I don't want you out in the streets late."

He reached into his pocket, pulled out a few bands and peeled off what he was taking with him.

"I'll be home later. Take this money with you put it in the stash," he instructed.

"I thought I was rolling with you tonight." She said with a slight attitude taking the money from his hand.

"Nah, I got shit I'm stepping into. I don't want you involved in it."

"Who's gonna have your back better than me?" she asked sticking the money down in her bag.

"You swear yo ass is a gangsta," Long laughed.

"Well, you trained me so what does that say about your G?"

"I'ma shut that mouth real good for you."

"That's what I want you to do," she got up and headed to the bathroom "You better step your game up playa."

Long smacked her ass. "You think you want it," he spat.

As she left the room, Naseem and Katina came back. Naseem was dressed in black from head to toe and strapped up. Long rose to his feet wearing his game face.

"Tell your girl don't forget what I told her," Long said to Katina as they prepared to leave.

When Breonni emerged from the bathroom the men were gone and Katina was sitting on the couch with a gloomy look on her face.

"What's wrong, Tina?"

"I get so scared sometimes when he leaves," she confessed.

"It's okay, mama. He got it," Breonni said. She sat beside Katina and pulled her girl's head to her chest. "Don't worry them niggas will be fine, they built for this shit."

Breonni tried to reassure her best friend but she had some of the same fears. All the words in the world could not sweet talk a bullet back into its chamber. All they could do was hope for the best and be prepared for the worst.

CHAPTER 22

Long Kiss...Good Night

Breonni spent several more hours at Katina's then headed home. Long was not there when she arrived. Even though he told her wouldn't be, she wanted to see him seated on the couch when she walked in. She locked the door, threw a slice of pizza in the microwave, and then moved into the bedroom. Breonni hit the lights and walked to the closet to stash the money that Long had given her.

Back in the kitchen, she took her pizza from the microwave and carried it back into the living room where she sat on the couch and channel surfed until her eyes became blurry. She forced herself to get up and shower then she jumped into bed.

Just when the sleep was getting good, Breonni was torn out of her slumber by the sound of furniture moving in the living room. Slowly, she sat up then eased off of the edge of the bed. She listened quietly as the sounds grew closer. Breonni slid the drawer next to the bed open and picked up the .22 and removed the safety.

Breonni tipped to the door and peeked out. She saw a

half-dressed Long leaning against the wall.

"What is the matter?" she asked.

She looked him over to see if he was hurt or injured. Before he could open his mouth to answer the question, the smell of liquor met her nose hard and strong.

"Damn, boy, what the fuck did you have?" she asked as he leaned forward resting the full weight of his body against her.

"Long, you're heavy. You gotta stand up," she said trying to prop him back against the wall.

"Why you got a gun, ma?" he asked pulling at her arm.

"Stop before you fuck around and kill both of us."

She wrinkled her brow as she slipped the safety back in place.

"Help me to the bathroom," he mumbled as his head rested against the wall.

Breonni shook her head and looked at him with disgust.

"Come on boy and don't talk in my face," she said. Breonni struggled to support his weight and to hold her breath at the same time.

Long leaned on Breonni as he tugged at his pants allowing them to fall to his ankles along the way. She helped him post up against the sink. Then, she set the shower to a comfortable temperature. When she turned around, Long was butt naked and giving her that fuck me gaze. She helped him up.

"Why you ain't got no clothes on?" he slurred tugging at her t-shirt as he stepped in the shower.

"I do have on clothes. Stop! Move your hands."

She tried to pull her shirt from his grip.

"Why you frontin'?"

He continued to grab at her shirt and her breasts. She pushed his hands away.

"Stop, Long! You're drunk and you're gonna get me wet."

"I wanna get you wet," he said pulling her into the shower.

"Long, baby, you're drunk and you trippin'."

She tried to assert herself as he grabbed her tightly in his arms and began kissing and biting her neck.

"Stop fighting this shit," he mumbled as he slid his hands between her thighs.

"Long," she called out. "Don't. Not like this, baby. Let me wash you up and help you to bed." She wanted to give him every part of her but she knew in his condition things were not going to go right.

"You know I love you," he whispered as he ran his hands all over her body.

"I know, baby. Come on let me get you straight so you can lay down,"

Long ignored her every plea as he forced his fingers deep inside her and stroked that spot just right.

Breonni was heating up and she knew that stopping him was not going to be an option so she surrendered.

The hot shower ran down over their bodies as he pulled her up to his waist and caressed her back.

"You know you gonna be mine forever no matter what, right?" he slurred as he continued to tickle her spot.

"Yes," she moaned as he nibbled on her erect nipple through the thin material of her t-shirt.

"Is this my pussy?' he mumbled as he gave the other nipple the same treatment.

"Yes," she whispered as she felt his thickness pulsating at the base of her pussy.

"You ready to give it to me?"

He looked up in her eyes for confirmation. The hot shower had sobered him up a bit but his drunken lust was in control of every move.

Unable to speak, Breonni nodded her head. Long stepped out of the shower with her legs wrapped firmly around his waist as he slightly staggered to his bedroom.

Breonni lay still as he began tracing his tongue all over her body. When he settled between her thighs she arched her back and enjoyed every lick and suck.

Long tasted her sweet nectar until she begged him to stop. When he rose up on his knees Breonni looked on through the slits of her eyes and fear set in.

"Long, please be gentle baby."

"Relax. You been dying to give me my pussy so open your legs wide and let me make you a woman," he ordered as he leaned in and covered her mouth with his.

The liquor on his breath and the lust in his eyes caused her to panic. Yes, she wanted him but not like this.

"Wait," she said and tried to push him off of her.

"We ain't waiting for shit."

Long grabbed her leg, pressed it to the bed, and slid inside her a few inches.

"Ohhh, Long, not like this."

She placed her hands on his chest and squirmed and wiggled as he slid in deeper.

"Relax and let me have what's mine," he grumbled as he pushed in and began slow stroking.

Breonni held on and closed her eyes tightly as he began

breaking her down inch by inch.

"Shit," Long moaned as her tightness squeezed him just right. Her wetness was calling his name and he answered with long deep strokes that made her back up with every entry.

"Don't run. This is what you been asking for. Take this dick."

He grabbed her wrists and pinned them to the bed picking up speed. Every moan and cry fueled his desire and increased the passion that sped through his body.

"Long, that's enough," she begged as he went deeper and deeper with every push.

"I'm just getting started," he said in her ear releasing her arms and grabbing one of her legs.

"Long! No!" Breonni pleaded.

He again ignored her. He was charged up and hitting the pussy like it had experience. Breonni bit down on her bottom lip and sunk her nails into his back as he pounded away without restraint. Her cries seemed to kindle his fire so she tried to be quiet and take it like a woman.

After he came, Long lay on top of her breathing heavily. Sweat ran from his body and settled into the crease of her breasts. Finally, he summoned enough energy to roll off of her, tucked a pillow under his head, and fell into a comatose sleep.

Breonni slowly moved her pain stricken body off the bed. She limped to the bathroom and quietly closed the door behind her. She cringed when her pee sent heat from her clit to her ass. Tears sprang into her eyes as she wiped away the bloody stickiness that had settled between her thighs.

Breonni flushed the toilet and washed her hands then ran herself a hot bath. Sliding her aching body into the steamy water, she desperately tried to erase the memory of what was more like rape than love. She never knew something she wanted so badly could cause so much confusion and pain.

She washed herself thoroughly, rinsed off and stepped into fresh pajamas. On her way to the guest room, she peeked in on Long. He was lying in the same position where she'd left him snoring peacefully. She tip toed to the guest room, crawled between the cool sheets, and covered her head with the pillow. Sleep eluded her. Instead, Breonni stayed up all night trying to convince herself that nothing had happened.

CHAPTER 23

Destruction

Shawn and Flint walked toward the White Castle on Elizabeth Avenue. They had pulled an all-nighter and wanted to grab some food before heading to the house.

"Yo, them New York bitches be wildin'," Flint slurred as he came around the truck.

"Man, when shorty squatted over that beer bottle, sucked that shit up, and squirted it in that nigga mouth, I almost gave her my whole fuckin' wallet," Shawn confessed as he pulled the door open.

"You crazy as hell," Flint laughed, stepping inside the restaurant behind him.

Hardly anyone was in line so their orders were filled quickly. Walking back to the car Flint had a bag full of food and was stuffing his mouth with a burger when he looked to his left and saw Shawn's sister posted up against a car with some dude all over her. He stopped dead in his tracks.

"Yo, my nigga ain't that Nadiyah?" he elbowed Shawn.

Shawn turned to see his fifteen-year-old sister all hugged

up with some nigga. He looked at his watch. Nadiyah should have been in school. Frowning, Shawn passed Flint his bag of food and stormed over in his sister's direction.

"Fuck is you doing out here?" he asked. Shawn stopped a foot in front of his sister and the random nigga. He scowled at ol' boy and thought about making the parking lot a crime scene.

Nadiyah's eyes bulged. She had not been expecting to see her brother.

"Shawn, I was on my way to school and I just stopped for something to eat," her voice trembled as she replied.

"It's ten o'clock. How the fuck you on your way to school?" he growled.

The dude's name was Kevin and he thought he was hard with his gangsta but Shawn could be a fool about his sister.

"Who this nigga?" Kevin tried to flex.

"Nigga, I'll blow your muthafuckin' head off," Shawn stepped closer to him.

Kevin bucked up.

"Wait. Kev, that's my brother," Nadiyah tried to step between them.

"Don't take up for this pussy ass nigga," Shawn barked moving her to the side.

"Shawn, please," she grabbed his arm.

"Go get in my truck before I slap the shit out of you," he ordered.

Nadiyah released his arm and headed in the other direction. When Flint saw his man all up in Kevin's face he headed towards them.

"This shit ain't worth it. Let's roll," Flint said as he put his hand to Shawn's shoulder.

Shawn took a few steps back holding eye contact with Kevin. Kevin wasn't backing down.

"Look, it's all peace. Just get in yo shit and go."

Flint tried to give Kevin a way out. Kevin held his gaze as he moved to his car and started it up. He was young but he was not a punk. He took in all of Shawn's features. He would see that nigga again and he wasn't going to let shit slide the next time he did.

When they got back to the truck, Shawn cussed Nadiyah out all the way to the school. When he let her out of the vehicle, she felt like a chastised kindergartner. She stomped up the steps of the school.

"I fucking hate him," she mumbled as she snatched open the doors and headed inside.

Nadiyah hid in the doorway and waited for them to pull away. She took out her cell phone and called Kevin. Within minutes, she was walking out the door and sliding into his passenger seat. Nadiyah was going to do what she was going to do.

* * * * *

"Baby, get ya phone," Jovanna called out as she glanced at the clock on the nightstand.

It was six o'clock A.M and Shawn was snoring. She shook him awake and handed him his Galaxy.

Shawn fumbled around and hit the call button. "Hello," he said as he turned over.

"Shawn, have you heard from your sister?" His mother's words jolted him wide awake.

"I saw her yesterday morning. Why?"

"She didn't come home last night and when I left this morning for work she still hadn't come home. I thought she may have been with you."

"Nah, but let me throw something on and go check some things out. I'll call you as soon as I find her."

"Okay, I will wait for your call." His mother hung up feeling sick to her stomach.

"Is everything okay?" Jovonna asked.

"I don't know yet. But I'll call you in a little while," he said.

Shawn threw on his clothes as fast as he could and headed to his mother's house. He called out for Nadiyah, but she didn't answer. He saw no evidence that she had even come home. He took out his cell phone and called her friend, Tracy. Her house was the usual cut spot. Teenagers would be there smoking and drinking all day. It was a rebellious teen's paradise filled with weed, food and chaos. The young boys loved it because they could fuck for free with no regrets. The young girls looked up to Tracy. They considered her hood royalty.

"Yo, Tracy. This Shawn," he said as soon as she answered the phone.

"Hey, boy, I haven't heard your voice in a minute."

"Have you seen Nadiyah?"

Shawn had no time for chitchat.

"She blew through here yesterday afternoon but I haven't seen her or Kev since then."

She sat forward rolling a blunt on her wooden coffee table.

"A'ight. Hit my phone if she blow through."

"Will do."

As soon as Tracy hung up, she dialed Damion.

"Speak," he answered.

"Get yo ass up nigga."

"What's good with you, ma?" Damion responded.

"He called me," she answered.

"Good. Is the nigga sweating?"

"He shook," Tracy reported with a sneaky smile on her face.

Damion thought about how they left Antwan's body in that ally.

"Yeah, them mufuckas touched the wrong niggas this time. Just make sure you watch the news," he said then disconnected the call.

Tracy put the blunt into her mouth. She relished thoughts of payback. Crossing her wasn't just the wrong move, it was a deadly one.

* * * * *

Shawn drove around the city for hours. He wracked his brain to think of places to look for Nadiyah. He didn't know that nigga, Kevin, so finding him was going to be hard. He tried to formulate his next move, but the streets weren't feeling him. Shawn hit one dead end after another. He had fucked up with a lot of niggas and the mere sight of him made them turn their heads.

He decided to go back to his mother's house to regroup.

Shawn entered the front door, turned off the alarm, and dropped his keys onto the glass coffee table. Exasperated, he sat down heavily on the white suede couch and laid his head back. He wanted to reach out to Naseem but the last thing he needed right now was his judgment.

CHAPTER 24

Terror

Hours later, Shawn sat in the same spot. When he looked up, his mom had arrived home. She walked in, took off her shoes at the door, and forced a smile to mask her uneasiness.

"Hey baby, I called you a few times but it went to your voice mail. Did you hear from your sister?" she asked as she came over to him and kissed his cheek.

"Not yet but you know how she do. How was your day?"

"Oh, it was tough, as usual. We have so many new clients and because I just made partner I had to oversee the new attorneys and they wore me out. I was lucky to get out when I did today," she said. "I wonder where your sister's at."

"Try to relax Ma. She'll pop up," he tried to comfort her.

"Relax? How am I going to do that without knowing where your sister's at?" she asked. "And, to make matters worse, I haven't heard from your father either. I don't know what to think."

Karen moved around the kitchen trying to busy herself.

"That girl's head is in a cloud. Some days I wish I could put her ass somewhere," Karen sighed as she pulled out pans and the ingredients to make a meal.

"Ma, it's gonna be alright. Nadiyah is probably hanging around with some of her friends."

From the living room, Shawn could see the worry on his mom's face. Age lines had formed around her pretty eyes seemingly overnight. Nadiyah was stressing her out. In a matter of months, her grades had dropped to below average and she had been arrested four times for shoplifting and disorderly conduct. She also had begun staying out to all hours of the night. The sudden change in her personality was destroying his mother.

Shawn again rested his head again and took a deep breath. He reached for his phone and dialed Naseem. After a few calls back to back went unanswered, he texted and placed the phone onto the table.

Karen ran water into a pot for the spaghetti, placed the pot on the stove, and then emptied the ground beef in a skillet. As she searched through the cabinet for seasonings she heard a loud knock on the door followed by a steady ringing of the bell.

Shawn went to the door. He looked back at his mom who stood at the island in the kitchen with a curious look on her face. Three police officers, two in plain clothes and one in uniform, were at the door.

"Are your parent's home? We have something to discuss with them," One of the officers said.

Shawn's heart dropped into his knees and his mouth became dry.

"Who is it, Shawn?" his mother called from the kitchen.

"It's for you," he yelled back.

"Please come in, officers."

When Karen saw the police officers, panic set in. She didn't know where to focus her energy. It was either her husband or daughter. Losing either of them would destroy her. Her knees got a little weak when she saw the stoic looks on the officers faces. She searched the eyes of the one officer she knew, Officer Craig, for a hint of the news that he was about to deliver.

Officer Craig walked over to her, put his hand on her shoulder, and said. "Karen, this is Detective Jordan and Officer Brown. We need you to come and identify a body."

Karen grabbed her chest and asked, "My daughter's or my husband's?"

"We would prefer you come down and see first."

He reached out to take her arm as she began to tremble.

"*My daughter or my husband?*" she cried out. Tears fell from her eyes as she backed away from him afraid to hear the answer.

"Karen, please calm down," Officer Craig said gently.

She snatched away from him. She took a few steps back and balled her fists at her sides.

"No! I'm not calming down. Tell me!" she screamed. Karen unclenched her fist and gripped the counter to keep from falling to the floor.

Officer Craig took a deep breath and said, "We think it's your daughter."

"Oh, God, nooooo! She sunk to the floor rocking back and forth. "Oh God, please no!" she wept.

Shawn felt like he had stepped out of his body. He

could see and hear but he couldn't move. Officer Craig went over to Karen, kneeled beside her, and put his arm around her.

"What happened, Craig?" she mumbled over and over again.

Just as the words was about to leave Craig's mouth Shawn looked up and saw his dad standing in the doorway. His face was still but his breathing was heavy. He dropped his lunch bag on the floor. When he saw that his wife was being comforted by his high school buddy, Officer Craig, his heart sunk and his chest ached.

"What's going on?" He managed to ask.

"Donald, someone killed our Nadiyah," Karen yelled out. As the words tumbled from her mouth, her lips started to quiver.

Donald looked at the officers and then back at Karen. He turned to look at Shawn with a pain in his eyes that was worse than death itself. Donald stood frozen in place as his keys slid from his hand and hit the floor. He grabbed his chest and started to hyperventilate. The strongest man Shawn had ever known gasped for air on the verge of a heart attack.

Donald fell backwards. He knocked a lamp off the end table as he crashed to the floor. The other two officers rushed to his side, tugged at his shirt, and ripped it open. Donald's body stiffened, shook, and then went limp. One officer immediately started to pump his chest while the other called over his radio for medical assistance.

Karen scrambled from Craig's grip and crawled over to her husband's side yelling, "Oh, God, no. Donald, please don't do this to me."

Tears fell from her eyes as she gripped the cuff of his pants tightly in her hands. Shawn couldn't move. His sister was dead. Now, his dad lay dying on the floor right before his eyes. The wail of ambulance's siren screamed loudly as it turned onto the block.

Seconds later, paramedics rushed in and whisked Donald out the door. Karen was carried to the hospital in a separate ambulance.

Shawn jumped into his car and raced to the hospital behind the emergency vehicles.

Donald was rushed through the doors right into surgery. Shawn lumbered into the emergency room like a zombie. He watched his mother laboring for air and staring at the ceiling with emptiness in her eyes. Tears slid down the side of her face as she squeezed the sheet firmly in her hand.

Shawn took a seat by her side and held her hand.

"Why is this happening to us?" his asked in a dry raspy voice.

Shawn shrugged and laid his forehead on his mother's hand. He had no answers, not for her nor for himself. When Karen was stable enough to move about, she was allowed to check on Donald.

A short while later, with Karen's condition improved, Officer Craig took her to the morgue for her to identify Nadiyah's body.

Shawn's shoulders slumped with defeat as he walked by his mother's side. Mother and son were led to a gurney where a body lay covered by a white sheet.

Shawn put his hand to his mouth as they got closer to the body. The smell was the worst he'd ever encountered.

He struggled not to throw up but when they uncovered the body he couldn't fight the inevitable. The sight of his sister's body sent him over the edge.

Karen's hands flew to her mouth and she let out a shrill cry. She was mortified. The sight of her baby girl in that condition almost made her pass out. Shawn had to steel himself to return to his mother's side. Karen's legs got weak and he hurried to support her. He put his arms around her and squeezed her tightly.

"Why they do this to my baby? What she do Shawn? What she do?" she cried.

Shawn held his mother in his arms as she sobbed deeply. He could feel her heart breaking and he knew that not even time would heal the gaping wound.

Karen stood at her daughter's side as if in a trance Shawn stepped to the side while his mother talked to Nadiyah as if she was still alive. His mouth filled with saliva and sweat beads spread across his forehead. He wanted to vomit again.

"I'll be right back, Ma," he whispered.

Karen just waved her hand and kept uttering incoherently.

Shawn walked down the hall to the water fountain. He wet his throat then leaned against the wall trying to get himself together. A short distance away, two female officers talked in low voices, but their words travelled down the hallway.

"Poor little girl, she was shot twice in the head. Then, they set her on fire. No one in the house survived. It appeared that she was in the wrong place at the wrong time," one of the officers said as they walked towards the exit.

Shawn stumbled over to a chair, collapsed from fatigue and turmoil, and cried.

The next couple of hours got even worse. Karen refused to leave her baby alone in the cold morgue. Officer Craig tried to comfort her while Shawn ran back and forth between the morgue and the operating room.

When Shawn returned to the morgue, his mother finally had left his sister's side.

"You ready to go upstairs?" he asked.

Karen remained silent. Shawn looked into her eyes and darkness peered back at him. He took her hand and led her to the elevator. When they returned to ICU, the doctor was looking around the waiting area. He looked up as they approached and met them halfway. Shawn feared that whatever he had to say would not be good.

"Mrs. McNeal," Dr. Sherman began in a comforting voice.

Karen had a blank look on her face. Her hair was all over the place. Her clothes looked as if she had slept in them for days and her dry, puffy eyes barely blinked.

"Your husband's heart failed two more times since your son left the floor. We checked his brain waves and they are non-responsive. It's like he has given up. We placed him on the ventilator until you returned."

Karen didn't have any energy left to even respond.

"We would like you to sign the paperwork to disconnect life support," the doctor advised.

Tears rolled down her face and a lump formed in her throat. Karen used what little energy she had left to push a few words from her mouth.

"Bring me the paperwork," she said coldly.

Within an hour, Karen had managed to sign away the lives of both her husband and her daughter. She knew that it would take years before she would even be able to pray to the God who'd forsaken her that day. Hesitantly, she walked into her husband's room. She looked at the tubes that were keeping Donald alive. Karen walked to his side, took his hand, and caressed her face with his palm.

"I hate that you're leaving me," she mumbled. "I don't want to do this without you."

Karen stroked his arm and their whole life together ran through her mind, from their first date to these final moments. She placed a single kiss on his hand and said her final goodbye.

"Hug and kiss our daughter for me," she whispered. The words felt like hot coals leaving her throat.

Shawn fought back the tears but what his body wanted to hold onto his heart let go. He raised his hand to his face and wiped away at the tears as soon as they tried to escape his eyes. His mother's world had come crashing down around her. He wished that he was lying dead in his sister's and father's place.

Karen placed Donald's hand on the bed when two nurses entered the room and began the process of disconnection. Karen laid her head onto his chest to listen to the final beats of his heart. When she could no longer hear the rhythm of his heart, she stood up and rubbed his head. Then, she allowed her body to collapse into the chair next to his bed.

Shawn sat next to his mother and held her hand. They looked at one another in paralyzing shock. Neither of them would be the same. When they laid Donald and Nadiyah to rest, Karen's and Shawn's souls were buried with them.

CHAPTER 25

A Living Hell

Months later…

T he winter months were hell for everyone in Naseem's crew. The same held true for some of their women. Spring was approaching along with Katina's due date. Naseem was handling every shipment with ease but was still cut out of the venture that KoKo assigned to Long. Baseem had advised him to keep moving product and get his weight up so she would have to respect his hustle.

Jovonna had almost completely withdrawn from her girls. She struggled under the weight of Shawn's depression.

Breonni had distanced herself from the team as well. Long was doing a little more than work in the streets and the rumors were weighing on her spirit.

Raven was caught between being with her man and tending to her sick father which kept her so busy that she felt like she was being ripped in two.

Katina felt the bond between friends deteriorating. She needed to do something to rekindle the connection. After days of begging, she finally had gotten Naseem to agree to allow her to throw a party at the Marriot hotel out by Newark International Airport.

"You know I'm not really feeling this shit, right?" Naseem said as she moved around their bedroom getting dressed. He stood in the mirror putting on his watch and jewels and looking at her with a stern eye.

"Babe, I know. But do this for me. I need this," she cooed. She moved over to him and wrapped her arms around his waist.

Naseem looked down at her bulging belly and wanted to call everything off, but he understood that it would upset her more than the reality that her friendships were falling apart.

He held her in his arms then released her with a warning, "If anything gets outta hand I'm snatching you up outta there, no questions asked. We clear?"

"Yes, we are clear. You so sexy in all this black," she quickly changed the subject. Reaching up on her tiptoes she kissed Naseem softly on his lips.

"Don't be trying to bribe me," he joked.

"I didn't do nothing."

Katina gave him her innocent look then pulled away from him to finish getting dressed.

Naseem smacked her butt as she walked away. Katina giggled as she moved to the bed to continue to get ready. He threw on his boots and headed to the living room. Katina pulled on her black jeans, a black thigh length loose fitting blouse and scented her skin. After sliding on a pair of red sling back three inch heels, she said a silent prayer, grabbed her clutch, and joined him in the living room.

Naseem tucked his gun in the small of his back then they headed for the car. They both had their doubts that this little party would bring everybody back together, but Katina was holding on to what little hope she had left.

"No matter what, I got you," he tried to reassure her. He could see the stress all over her pretty brown face.

"I know."

Pulling into the Marriot, heaviness weighed in her chest. She looked over at Naseem and feigned a smile.

"You straight?" he asked picking up on her apprehension.

"Yeah, I'm good." Katina tried to convince him but she wasn't really convinced herself.

As they entered, they heard the music knocking. A sea of people rocked to the beat of *Work* by ASAP ferg.

I'ma pimp though, no limp though,
couldn't copy my style in Kinkos
Put in work, run up on a killer then I put him in the dirt
Run up in the buildin', semi gon' squirt,
that's what a nigga get when they gettin' on my nerves
I ain't lyin' - lay 'em on the curb,
ridin' on a killer who be coming at Ferg!
(Damnnnnnnnn!) Girl you twerk,
twerk that kitty girl make it purr
Put in work, Flacko put 'em in the dirt.

Katina bobbed her head to the beat. Naseem was tense. He was especially uneasy because she was so far along in her pregnancy. Besides he just didn't do crowds. Katina felt his grip tighten on her hand with every step.

Katina looked up at him she could tell he was ready to go even though they had just got there. She rubbed his arm and tried to ease his mind. She at least wanted to see her girls before he ushered her back to the car.

Katina scanned the room and when her eyes settled to the roped off area in the back she saw Long and Flint and several dudes they associated with. She gently pulled Naseem in their direction.

Walking up towards security, she excitedly threw up her VIP pass.

"Hey, sis."

Long stood up to greet Katina. Like Naseem, he was dressed in all black with his jewels shining.

"Hey, yourself. Where is Bre?" Katina asked looking around.

"She's around here somewhere. You know your girl."

Katina turned to Flint and asked, "Where is Raven?"

"She's on her way. She slow as hell, you know ya girl."

He stood up and kissed her cheek and rubbed her stomach.

"We almost done, huh?" Flint asked smiling from ear to ear.

"Yes, thank God. But I hear you just getting started. Congrats," she tried to relay over the music.

"Thanks, little sis," he replied full of pride.

"Where is Shawn and JoJo?"

"I don't know. I haven't seen them," he forced his voice over the music.

Katina began to feel a little sick and her spirits were down because her girls weren't near her. Only a few minutes into the evening, disappointment reigned.

"What you drinking, nigga?"

Hammer came over and hit palms with Naseem.

"I ain't fucking around tonight. I gotta be on point," he said as they bumped shoulders.

"I hear you. I'll handle your share," he said, taking a bottle to his mouth and turning it all the way up. Hammer was one shade from pitch black and sported all black. If it wasn't for his teeth, that nigga would have been damned near invisible.

Naseem chuckled as he took a seat and pulled Katina onto his lap. She ordered a glass of orange juice from the waitress and scanned the crowd. Her eyes bounced between the bar and the door. When she looked over and saw Breonni all in some nigga's face, she almost pissed her pants. Long was catching the same shit she had just caught.

Long became more agitated by the second. He sipped his drink and watched Breonni through squinted eyes as she worked her way through the crowd. She was stopped by different niggas along the way. She was drunk and loud by the time she made her way to the VIP.

"Hey, Tina," she yelled out.

She fell a little to the side. Long grabbed her arm to hold her up. Breonni gave him a dirty look and pulled away.

"Hey, mama."

"What's up, Naseem? Why you looking at me all up and down?" Breonni asked.

"You need to sit yo drunk ass down somewhere," he said. Naseem couldn't act like the shit wasn't happening.

Breonni flailed her hands at him and said, "Whatever. I came out to have a good time and I plan on doing just that."

She reached over and grabbed Long's drink spilling it in the process.

Long was heating up faster than mercury but he tried to remain calm.

"I'm about to take you home."

"Ah, no you're not."

"Let me holla at you for a minute."

Long jumped up, snatched the drink from her hand, and slammed it onto the table. Gritting his teeth, he grabbed her arm and moved her quickly towards the lobby.

"Why are you grabbing on me?" Breonni protested as she was marched outside.

She slipped and slid on her heals trying to resist but he just kept pulling her towards the door. Heads were turning as Long dragged her through the parking lot.

"Nas, I gotta go talk to her."

Katina shot up and moved swiftly. Naseem stood up and followed her.

They found Long and Breonni outside, standing between two cars shouting at one another.

"Bre," Katina yelled as she pushed through the doors.

"Not now, Tina," she said then went back in on Long. "So, what the fuck you sayin'?"

"I'm not doing this shit with you. I need you to get ya shit and get the fuck out my house." He tried to walk away but she grabbed the back of his shirt.

"You putting me out? Why? So you can put the next bitch in my spot?" she yelled pulling at his clothes.

"Look, yo ass is drunk and I am trying not to go the fuck off. Let me go," he said as calmly as possible.

"You ain't shit!" Breonni pushed him in chest.

The evidence of his infidelity had been weighing heavily on her heart. Instead of confronting him, she began to drink and party to ease her pain. Tonight she showed her ass in rare form. Long got into her face.

"Don't ever put your fucking hands on me again," he growled.

"What? You wanna put your hands on me now?" She stared up in his eyes with intensity.

For a quick moment Long saw himself knocking her head clean off her shoulders but that wasn't his style. He forced a smirk on his face.

"Nah, I'm good. You're gonna destroy yourself. In fact, you already fucked up."

He walked back towards the hotel.

Breonni took off after him screaming, "Yeah, I might be fucked up, but blame that shit on yourself. Like I don't know about them other bitches."

She caught up to him and grabbed the back of his shirt. Long snatched away but eyed her fiercely.

"I swear on everything I love, if you touch me again, I am going to wake up with a lot to regret. Stay the fuck away from me," he warned.

"Fuck you! You sorry muthafucka," she spat.

Long looked at her pitifully. She had lost all her shine. The person she was to him no longer existed. He didn't even know who this new person was. When he turned to walk away again Breonni flew after him in rage. Katina quickly stepped between them.

"Move, Tina," Breonni cried as she tried to get around her.

"No, you need to act like you got some sense. What the hell is wrong with you?" she yelled in her face.

"You on his side, Tina?" Breonni asked.

She felt a sharp pain in her chest. In their ten years of friendship, they had never fought or argued.

"I am on the side of right. And right about now, you're wrong as hell." Katina was breathing heavily and on the verge of slapping Breonni herself.

A small crowd had gathered around. Tears welled up in Breonni's eyes and embarrassment began to replace her anger.

"You need to take yourself home and sleep it off before you do something you will regret," Katina advised.

"It's too late for that. I already regret everything about this night including standing here talking to you." She paused. "Yeah, I think I better leave before I say something I can't take back."

She backed up slowly then turned and walked away.

"Bre. Bre!" Katina yelled but she kept on walking.

"Stop yelling, ma, and come on." Naseem said.

"I can't let her walk down the darn highway in the middle of the night."

"Don't worry. I got her."

Naseem turned to Hammer who had come out to see what was going on and ordered him to get Breonni and take her wherever she wanted to go.

"This mess is crazy. Take me home," Katina said to Naseem. Anger flooded her body.

"A'ight."

Naseem walked her to the car then went back inside to secure everything. When he got back to the car, tears were rolling down Katina's face. Not only had she lost her temper, she had lost her best friend.

* * * * *

"That's the nigga we been looking for right there," Paco stated pointing at Naseem's car as it pulled out of the parking lot.

"Get the fuck outta here," his boy spat sitting up in the car to get a better look.

"Yeah, that's him." He nodded as he thought back to how dirty they did Antwan. "Follow that nigga. I need to see where he rest his head."

Paco's boy followed Naseem at a safe distance. When they pulled into his parking space outside of his apartment, they parked and watched Naseem and Katina emerge from the car.

"You want me get that nigga?" his boy asked reaching down under the seat.

"Nah, be cool," Paco said. His eyes remained fixed on his target. "I got some real special plans for him and his whole team. Let's go."

An evil scowl formed on his face and the sweet taste of payback tickled his tongue.

CHAPTER 26

Regret

Following the party, things got progressively worse. Breonni was forced to move back home. Because of what Long had done to Mike, he and her mother tortured her verbally and emotionally every day. It was like she was in hell with the fire on blast. Katina tried to reach out to her but Breonni would not accept her calls.

After the tragedy that hit Shawn and his family, he had become a complete liability. Naseem and Long stopped fucking with him on business altogether. They could not afford to risk what they built by dealing with his instability.

Instead of pushing away from Shawn, Jovonna became his crutch staying close to his side and closing herself off from the world.

Raven was the only one who maintained any communication with Katina. Even so, since she had just learned she was pregnant, she stuck even closer to Flint.

* * * * *

It was a hot Saturday night. Summer was fast approaching. Long, his new lady, Vera, Naseem, and Katina decided to catch a movie at Jersey Garden Mall. Katina was getting in her last hurrah before welcoming their son into the world.

They had just exited the theater when they noticed Breonni coming out of the bathroom. When she saw them coming her way, she threw on a phony smile.

"Hey, Katina," she said.

Breonni gave her a hug and rubbed her belly.

"You look like you ready to pop."

"Hey, Bre. Who you here with?" she asked.

She noticed a bruise under Breonni's eye.

"Oh. I'm here with a friend. What's up, big bruh?" she asked Naseem as she gave him a hug.

"I'm good, little mama. How you?"

Breonni cut her eyes at Long and noticed Vera on his arm. She looked her up and down disapprovingly.

"How you doin', Bre?" Long asked with sincerity.

This was the first time they had seen each other since she moved out. He had been hearing rumors that the nigga she was with was putting his hands on her and that bruise on her face was confirmation.

"I'm good," she replied avoiding eye contact.

"Let me holla at you for a minute."

Long took her arm and led her to the side.

"Excuse me," Vera said folding her arms.

Long didn't respond. He looked at her with a raised eyebrow then turned his attention back to Breonni.

"If you ever need anything, I'm here," he said.

"All I ever needed from you was for you to love me and not treat me like a jump-off."

"You know I got mad love for you. And…"

"Bre!" a voice bellowed from behind her.

Breonni's head snapped around and panic flashed in her eyes. Bishop walked over to them, put his arm over Breonni's shoulder, and pulled at her neck.

"Who is this?" he asked as he locked eyes with Long.

"I'm just a friend," Long said.

"She don't need no fucking friends," Bishop shot back.

"Baby, he's just somebody from around the way," she tried to comfort Bishop.

"I don't give a fuck!"

He raised his voice causing the other three cats that were with him to perk up.

Naseem tensed up and moved forward. He saw bulge in Bishop's shirt and tried to quickly defuse the situation. The last thing he wanted was something to pop off with Katina with him.

"It's all good. Let's bounce, my nigga," he instructed Long.

Long threw his hands up.

"I'll catch you next time little mama," he said to Breonni.

Bishop was drunk and wanted to make a scene. Long knew that if he put the nigga on his ass he would take it out on Breonni later.

"Call me, Bre," Katina said as she was led away by Naseem.

Long took Vera's hand and they all left the theater.

* * * * *

It had begun to rain. Bishop's foul mouth was ripping Breonni's spirit to shreds. She tried to tune him out but she choked back tears. She had managed to do everything she said she would never do. She had put a man between her and Katina. She also had put a wedge of fear and lies between them that she didn't know how to remove.

Bishop fussed and drove recklessly. Breonni snapped out of her thoughts and gripped the door handle glaring at him. When he almost hit a parked car, she screamed.

"What are you doing?" her voice was thick with hatred and anger.

Bishop came to a stop at a traffic light. He slowly turned to look at her. Then, he punched her in the face. Breonni's head smacked against the window.

"Don't you ever disrespect me again, bitch!" he barked.

He swerved left and right as he pulled off again.

Breonni raised her hand to her face. Her eye felt like it was swelling fast and she heard ringing in her ears.

"Got niggas all in your fucking face like you ain't got no man. What the fuck is wrong with you?" Bishop yelled and his fist slammed into her face again.

The car swerved hard to the right barely missing a mailbox as he jumped the curb. Breonni was too terrified to cry out for fear of upsetting him more.

When he pulled up to the house Breonni was shaking. She peeked at him out of the corner of her swollen eye. The rain beat down on the car. She opened the car door and struggled up the walkway in the pouring rain.

Once inside, Bishop started apologizing. Breonni stood

quietly. Her wet clothes clung to her body. Hot tears cascaded down her face.

Bishop stared at her with pleading eyes. Then he was on her. He planted foul, sloppy kisses all over her face. When his mouth met hers she thought she would lose her guts.

"You know I love you, right?" he asked looking at her through the slits of his blood red eyes.

"Yes."

"Why you always making me hurt you?" he asked.

Bishop worked his hands down into her jeans and up her blouse at the same time. Breonni closed her eyes. Her skin crawled with every touch.

"Come. Let me get some pussy and make it up to you," he said as he pulled her towards the room.

Breonni surrendered to what had become a routine. Bishop would get pissy drunk then make up reasons to fight her. When he was done using her for a punching bag, he would rip at her clothes and force himself inside her and pump away angrily until he came. Then, he would fall asleep. Tonight would be no different.

She tried to pretend she wasn't there while Bishop pumped and moaned and gave her drunk, wet kisses. Breonni filled her mind with thoughts of Katina and the baby or the sound of the laughter they had shared as girls. This brought a little joy to her heart.

Breonni was brought back to the here and now when she heard him say, "Fuck me, bitch." Bishop smacked her ass and tugged at her waist forcing her to push back on all that dick while he held her in place and pushed in harder with every thrust. She pushed back and cried with every painful stroke.

When he began to cum he grunted and moaned like a wild animal releasing then falling to the side. Breonni fell forward and grabbed the sheets to quickly cover her shame. She hated who she had become.

She had been rescued from a violent, drunken situation to only fall into an even worse one. The vow she made to herself to never be her mother had been shattered into pieces with every forceful blow from Bishop's fist.

"Move over, bitch. It's hot," were the last words she heard before the sickening sound of him snoring filled the room.

Breonni lay still until she felt it safe to move then eased off of the bed. She tiptoed to the bathroom and gently closed the door. She turned on the water sat on the toilet and cried from her soul. *Why me?* She asked herself.

After she took a shower she stepped out and put on her pajamas. Flashes of Long crowded her thoughts as she ran a comb through her hair. She wiped the mirror and looked at her swollen, bloodshot eye. Again, tears ran down her face. She turned her face from side to side and examined her bruises. She hardly recognized the reflection in the mirror.

Her life had been turned inside out. The laughter was gone. It had been replaced with emptiness. *This life*, she thought, *isn't worth living*.

CHAPTER 27

I Got You

Around three-thirty in the morning Long was torn out his sleep by a bang at the door. He glanced around the room. He looked at the clock and then at Vera who was fast asleep. He thought that he may have been dreaming but the banging started again. He jumped up, threw on his sweat pants and grabbed his gun. He quickly moved through the living room in the dark and went for the door.

"Who is it?"

"It's Breonni."

Long removed the chain and locks and slowly opened the door. Breonni stood their soaking wet in her pajamas with her head down.

"I didn't know where else to go," she said as the tears rolled down her face.

"Come in, ma."

He checked to make sure she was alone. Breonni came in and stood by the door like a scared child. Long turned on the light. When he saw her face he wanted to go off.

He lay his gun down on the table and lifted her chin so he could get a better look.

"What the fuck?" he said as he tried to remain calm. "That nigga hit you because of me didn't he?"

Breonni nodded her head up and down.

"I'ma kill that pussy."

He let her go, snatched up his gun, and turned towards the bedroom to get dressed.

"Long please don't," Breonni said and grabbed his arm.

He saw fear in her eyes. That's something he had never seen in her before. Long realized he needed to get her straight first then deal with that nigga. He put down the gun and tried to settle down.

"Come here."

He took her into his arms and held her tightly.

"I'm sorry this happened to you. I got you. You can stay with me as long as you need to."

Even as he tried to comfort Breonni, Long started to devise a plan to rock Bishop's world.

Breonni's wet body rested against Long's and she melted in the security of his embrace. For the first time in weeks, she felt at peace.

Long reassured her that everything was going to be okay. He gave her a big t-shirt and took her to the bathroom to get cleaned up. When he looked and saw old and new bruises all over her body, the rage came back. Breonni looked down in shame.

"It's okay, ma. I'm not judging you," he assured her.

"I fucked up," she admitted.

"You gonna be alright. Let me get you straight, ma."

Long ran her a tub of hot water and helped down into it. He sat on the edge of the tub rubbing the cloth over her aching body as she released portions of her pain. Long listened to her recounting of the beatings she had taken and how she felt like shit about losing her friends.

"I'm sorry I turned on you," she acknowledged wiping the tears from her eyes.

"You don't owe me an apology. I owe you one. I fucked up what we had but, don't worry, I got you."

Long rubbed his hand over her head then leaned in to kiss her bruised cheek. Breonni didn't respond. She just pulled her knees up to her chest, rested her forehead on them, and sobbed. After she was bathed, he covered her with his robe led her to the couch to sit down. He made her a hot cup of tea and sat beside her.

"I'm sorry for everything," he apologized.

"It's my fault. I didn't trust you. And, it put a wedge between us."

Long looked at this beautiful woman, beaten and broken, and felt responsible for some of her pain. The only thing he could do to make things right was to make sure she was safe.

"Let me get some things straight right quick so you can get some rest."

Long gave her a half smile. Breonni weakly returned the smile and sat back to finish her tea. Long went to wake Vera.

"Baby, I need you to go home," he said as she shook her leg.

"What?" Vera looked at him like he was crazy for waking her up in the middle of the night.

"I got some shit I have to handle. I'll hit you up tomorrow."

He turned on the light as he gathered her things and helped her out the bed.

"Long, what is going on?" she asked as she dressed.

"I'll explain it to you later."

He grabbed his phone and called a cab.

"I need you to talk to me *now*."

She crossed her hands over her chest as she stood in the middle of the floor.

"And I said we will deal with it tomorrow. Now finish getting dressed."

Vera remained still for a minute and then she resumed dressing. Long grabbed a knot and handed it to her. Vera snatched it from his hand and plopped on the bed. Rage coursed through her veins.

An uneasy silence filled the room. Vera was afraid to ask questions and Long was praying she didn't start no shit and make an already difficult situation even worse. Vera couldn't take it anymore. She needed to know what she had done to get put out of his bed in the middle of the night.

"So what is this about? What did I do to deserve this Long?" she asked.

"Nothing. I told you I have to take care of something,"

Vera was unsatisfied with his response and just as she was about to go in for her second round she heard a horn blowing outside.

"Come on."

Long jumped up and grabbed her purse from the dresser handed it to her and headed toward the door. Vera grabbed her cell from the nightstand and followed him. When she saw Breonni sitting on the couch in Long's robe with a towel wrapped around her head drinking tea, Vera caught an attitude. Long rushed her out the door before she could get started.

"You ain't shit," Vera spat as he ushered her down the steps.

"I will talk to you tomorrow."

"Fuck you! Go talk to that bitch."

Vera snatched away from his grip and yanked the cab door open. Long put her into the cab and shut the door. He remained calm despite her attitude. The situation was fucked up enough and he didn't want to add salt to her wounds.

He felt Vera's pain but the woman he owed his comfort to tonight was on the other side of his door. This time he was not going to let her down.

When he returned to the apartment, Breonni was sitting on the couch still in a daze. He came and took her hand and gently pulled her to her feet. She kept her head down as he tried to lead her to the bedroom.

"I can sleep out here. I don't want to inconvenience you," she said a little over a murmur looking back at the couch.

"Ma, I got you."

He reached his hand out and turned her face towards his. Breonni quickly dropped her head.

"Don't look at me, Long."

"Baby," he said lifting her chin. "You still my pretty Breonni. I just have to renew your spirit."

Long leaned in and kissed her swollen eye.

"Come lay with me. Let me hold you tonight."

He took her hand firmly in his and led her to the guest bedroom.

Breonni cheered up a little when she saw that the room was the same way she left it. Her perfume and lotion were still in place on the dresser and slippers next to the bed. He released her hand and lay on the bed and opened his arms.

"Come mere," he summoned her.

Breonni crawled next to him as he pulled her body close to his. "No worries. I got you. And that nigga gotta die. You already know. Get some rest, baby."

Breonni snuggled against him and prayed for Bishop's death to be long and painful. Long held her tightly until he heard her breathing become heavy. Then, he, too, dozed off.

CHAPTER 28

Let Me Ease Your Pain

Long was on the hunt for Bishop. He had sprinkled money all over town and was still coming up empty. He knew it was only a matter of time before the nigga would slip up. Still, he was frustrated that the slimy bastard had been eluding him.

Meanwhile, Long and Naseem had gotten an invitation to meet with Baseem out of town. They were about to get the break they needed to expand. Long went straight home to prepare for the trip. Breonni placed his clothes in a duffle bag and collected his toiletries from the bathroom while he sat counted money and made a few phone calls.

"I'll only be gone for a couple days. I want you to stay at the house. Do not leave."

He walked over to the closet, got his extra gun and gave to her.

"I taught you how to use this. If a nigga come up in here, air his ass out and if he's still alive the cops can ask him all the questions they want to."

"Thank you for everything."

She gave him a little smile then dropped her head. She still was not able to make full eye contact.

"No, thank you. I love you."

He pulled her into his arms placing his lips on hers and gave her a single kiss.

"See you in a couple days."

"I love you more. Be careful," she said.

Long winked at her and was out the door.

Breonni sat on the bed and looked at the phone. She wanted to call Katina but she was too ashamed. She decided to let a little more time pass. Then, she would swallow her pride and make the call. While Long was away, Breonni busied herself cleaning the house from top to bottom. She even organized Long's closet by colors. Once she got busy, the week seemed to fly by.

Long returned from his trip feeling happy but worn out. The meeting was everything he hoped for and more. Kayson had some enemies he needed handled and if Naseem and he could get it done cleanly and quickly, their blessings would be plentiful. Long checked the area then jumped out and grabbed his bag from the back seat.

When Breonni heard the keys she got excited. She was sitting on the couch in her stretch pants and t-shirt finishing her meal and watching old repeats of Martin.

"Hey, baby," he said as he set his bag down.

"Hey, you."

She rose to her feet empty plate in one hand and glass in the other.

"How was your trip?"

"I made it back."

He gave her a smile.

"You ain't make me nothing?" he asked walking further into the living room.

"You should have called. But I can go and make you something."

She turned real fast to go to the kitchen.

"Nah. I'm good. Relax."

"You sure?"

"Yeah, I was just teasing. Let me get situated then I'll be back to chill with you."

"Okay," she replied then went into the kitchen to wash the dishes.

Breonni reached over and turned on the radio and began to sing along with K. Michele V.S.O.P as she dried and put away the pots. *"We gon' do whatever you like. Very special. Got some Henney chillin' on ice. Very special."* She pouted her lips and sang into a wooden spoon.

Long returned to the kitchen to see her still at the sink with all her curves on full display as she swayed to the music. Walking up behind her, he put his hands on her shoulders causing her to almost jump out of her skin.

"Hold up baby. It's me."

"You scared me."

She quickly turned away from him. Long looked her. She had once been supremely confident. Now she was broken and afraid. He reached out and took her trembling hands into his.

"What did he do to you?" he asked in a very low tone.

Breonni took a deep breath.

"He took everything that I was," she replied in a whisper as tears slid down her face.

Long took her into his arms pressing her tear stained face against his chest.

Breonni rested against him looking up with grief stricken eyes. Long kissed her face and lips tenderly. She lowered her lids and melted to his touch.

"I never gave him what I have for you," she said softly.

"I know."

He palmed her butt firmly in his hands and kissed her like it was their first time.

"Can I make love to you?"

"Yes, I need you," she whispered.

Long picked her up in his arms. Breonni nestled her nose in his neck inhaling his scent.

Standing next to the bed Long stared down at her with tender eyes.

Breonni looked to the floor.

"Baby, you can't hide from me. I see you."

He pointed at her heart then slowly lifted her chin to look into her eyes. Their eyes connected. This time, Breonni allowed him into her soul.

"I'ma go real slow. You want me to stop, just let me know," he stated, placing a single kiss on her lips.

Breonni nodded her head as his hands began to explore her small frame.

Long took his time with every piece of clothing. He stopped to admire each part of her body: her toes, her ankles, her calves, her knees. He worked his way up her body gracing each body part with gentle kisses. He lay her down in the middle of his bed and admired the sweet plumpness between her thighs. Long ran his tongue from her ankle to her inner-thighs. Breonni jumped.

"Baby, you don't have to."

She pulled at his arm to bring him to her.

"This is long overdue, ma. Let me make you feel good tonight."

He lowered himself between her legs and began to lap at her clit with the tip of his tongue. Breonni's body responded just like he wanted it to. Her hips gyrated as she flooded his mouth with sticky pleasure. Long glanced up and got charged as he saw the passion all over Breonni's face. She moaned even louder as his tongue slid up and down her lips.

"Ssss."

She moved her head from side to side.

"Baby," she called out lustfully.

Long placed his mouth over her clit. He worked his magic, sucking hard then softly, lifting her higher and higher.

When her body started to jerk he said, "Come for me, baby."

Long sucked her essence until she trembled squirming out of his arms while clutching the sheets tightly. Breathing heavily and shivering, Breonni tried to recover.

Long planted soft kisses as he worked his way up her stomach. He sucked at her nipples causing her to squirm.

"Mmmm, baby," she moaned as he bit softly on her neck.

As he entered her, Breonni caressed Long's back with her fingertips. He pulled back a bit offering short, slow strokes. His tongue explored her mouth. They moved together, cheek to cheek, and he moaned in her ear as her muscles squeezed his dick.

"You're gonna make me go deep."

"I need you to go deep," she moaned.

Breonni gripped his ass to force him deeper inside her.

Long gave in to whatever he felt would make her feel better. He was rewarded with her sexy cries, wet lips, and complete openness.

They had been together many times, but for the first time they were connected. It felt as though their souls were joined as one. Neither of them had ever felt that before.

Breonni moved in perfect rhythm under his strength. She gave him the parts of her heart that she always feared to share. She released to him that which no man had ever touched. She knew from this day forward she would worship the ground he walked on. She would worship the ground he walked upon not because the dick was good but because the heart attached to it was golden.

CHAPTER 29

Tainted

Glen's cancer got progressively worse. Although Flint was against it, Raven continued to go to her father's house to clean and cook his meals. Her father was the only parent she had growing up. Turning her back on him was not an option for her.

Raven prepared Glen's breakfast and lunch for the next day like she always did. Then, she cleaned the kitchen and bathroom and went to her old room to look for some important papers.

Raven fumbled through a few envelops, perplexed as to where she had put everything. She turned to go back to her dresser drawer to re-check it and was startled. When she looked up, Glen stood in the doorway half dressed.

"So, you're gonna let me taste you tonight?" he asked with a lustful and evil gleam in his eye.

Confused and afraid, Raven stood next to her dresser. She lowered her tear-filled eyes.

In a low, trembling voice she answered. "I don't think that we should do that anymore, Daddy."

"What the fuck you mean we can't do that anymore?" The anger in his voice cased her body to quiver.

Raven plucked up the courage to respond, "It's not right and it has to stop."

In a flash, Glen smacked her upside the head knocking her backward. Raven hit the wall hard and slid to the floor. Whimpering, she crawled to the nearest corner and covered her head. Glen stalked over to her and began punching her in the head and arms.

"Nooo, please!" Raven cowered in the corner.

"It's that nigga, ain't it?" he shouted.

He attempted to pull her head from between her knees. Glen towered over her in rage at the thought of her turning him down.

"No. I swear, Daddy. I haven't let him come between us," she cried.

"You gave that nigga my pussy?" he fumed.

Raven was too afraid to speak. The longer silence ruled the room the angrier he became.

"Oh, you ain't got shit to say? I know what will make you talk."

Glen turned suddenly and left the room.

Quickly, Raven scrambled for her phone. Her heart raced with fear for the baby growing inside her as well as herself.

"Hello," the voice of her savior came through the phone.

"Please come and get me," she whispered as she watched the door for her father's return.

"Raven, what's wrong?"

"Please, hurry! I think he's going to kill—"

The call disconnected.

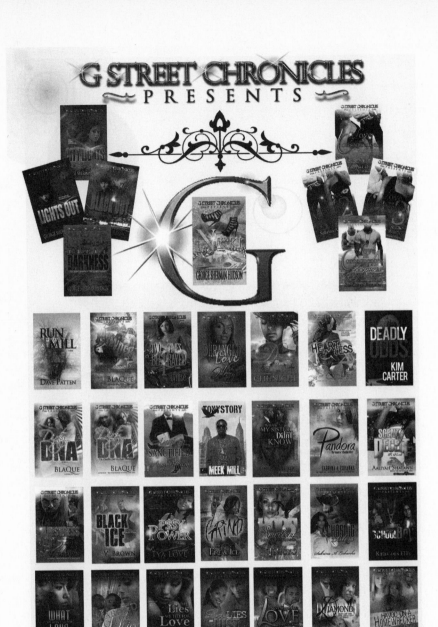

Hunger, greed, addiction and lust can always stand in the way of success. I Used To Love Her is a hip-hop love drama full of lies, deception and murder. Trey Eight, a budding rap star and member of the group Hustle Kingz, struggles to claw his way to the top with treachery lurking around every corner.

Annie Oakley knows all too well about the hard road to success. The transition from lamb to wolf is the only transition one can make to stay afloat in this industry, and when all else fails she uses what she's got to get what she wants. She knows that everybody loves a star when they're on top, but in order to maintain that top spot and keep the crowd chanting your name one has to be more grimy than the next man or woman.

Climb into the pages of I Used To Love Her and take this journey into the world of love, hate, power and hip-hop.

We'd like to thank you for supporting G Street Chronicles
and invite you to join our social networks.
Please be sure to post a review when you're finished reading.

Like us on Facebook
G Street Chronicles
G Street Chronicles CEO Exclusive Readers Group

Follow us on Twitter
@GStreetChronicl

Follow us on Instagram
gstreetchronicles

Email us and we'll add you to our mailing list
fans@gstreetchronicles.com

George Sherman Hudson, CEO
Shawna A., COO